Praise for
Filthy Sucre

Ghosh's prose, as ever, is unique, vivid, lyrical and clever. This trio of novellae is like sipping a fine wine – scintillating, rich, and lingering long after one sets it down. Take your time. You are about to read flash at its best.

~ Eileen Merriman, author of *Pieces of You, Catch Me When You Fall* and *Moonlight Sonata*

From the limitless imagination of Nod Ghosh, we readers are gifted with three novellas of impressive scope and depth. These narratives, deftly distilled and interwoven, speak to the vagaries of love and loss, of betrayal and intrigue. Brilliant, dark, and riveting, *Filthy Sucre* is a collection by one of our best writers at the height of her powers.

~ Kathy Fish, author of *Wild Life: Collected Works from 2003-2018*

Nod Ghosh knows how to unspool a tale that keeps us turning pages, missing train stops, and binge-reading way into the night. The three flash novellas of *Filthy Sucre* entice us into complex liaisons both acrid and sweet; to read her work is to become complicit in her clever webs of dysfunction, where guilt and innocence lose their boundaries and human nature is laid bare.

~ Nancy Stohlman, author of *Madam Velvet's Cabaret of Oddities* and *The Vixen Scream and other Bible Stories*

Nod Ghosh creates imaginary worlds filled with deliciously messy love. Her writing moves us through humor and heartbreak, weaving comedy and tragedy together seamlessly. Anything but simple, her characters haunt us, worry us, thrill us – and remind us of what it is to be painfully alive.

~ Meg Pokrass, author of *Damn Sure Right*, *Alligators at Night* and *The Dog Seated Next to Me*

Just when you think flash fiction has got as big as it's possible to get, along comes *Filthy Sucre* and blows all your expectations out of the water. These three very different novellas-in-flash take the reader everywhere and everywhen moving through narrative universes populated with characters so real and flawed and complicated, they leap right off the page and into your mind. This is novella-in-flash at its best – each tiny story complete in itself but when read together the effect is exponential.

~ Jan Kaneen, author *The Naming of Bones*

A heartbreaking and epic trio of novellas, *Filthy Sucre* ushers us into worlds of complex and confounding relationships through a rich cast of characters full of love and hurt. As the three very different stories race along, character decisions twist and contort their experience of life, and as a reader, you can't help but marvel and question your own experience: What does it mean to be 'in relationship'? What responsibility do we have to our true selves and to each other? How much of our experience of life is free will and how much is inescapable destiny?

~ Jenna Heller, joint winner of the 2019 *Meniscus* prize for prose

In *Filthy Sucre*, Nod Ghosh paints fresh and stinging portraits of human vulnerability and fallibility. The three novellas will pull you fully into the worlds of her characters, mixing lush details with harsh surroundings, tragedy with amusement, and surreal happenings with all-too-familiar human experiences. Ghosh's highly flawed and unforgettable protagonists will keep you thinking about them long after the final line.

~ Charmaine Wilkerson, author of *How to Make a Window Snake*

The three novellas-in-flash collected together in *Filthy Sucre* span the breadth and depth of time, space, and emotion. From adulterous men and ill-fated lovers to benign deities, these flashes enthral and alarm in Ghosh's signature voice. Each reader will have their favourite novella from this volume; the aftermath of a disappearance in *Another Silent Movie* held me in suspense and awe. Whichever your favourite, you'll want to read all of Ghosh's compelling stories again and again.

~ Santino Prinzi, author of *This Alone Could Save Us*

As binge-worthy as anything on Netflix, you'll only mistake this collection for a quick read until the poetic nuggets start hitting you right between the eyes. These novellas echo and bounce off each other, full of mystery, heartbreak, beauty, and the sheer gnarliness of being human. Having drawn these awful, gorgeous characters, Ghosh is a tender observer of people being kind and brave, rebelling, giving in, and doing some very shitty things to each other.

~ Zoë Meager, winner of the Commonwealth Writers Short Story Prize, Pacific Region, 2013

Filthy Sucre is a collection of three flash fiction novellas. Each story in each section stands alone, but there are connecting threads throughout that advance the reader's understanding of the characters and the situations in which they find themselves. The themes are woven around lost love, lost trust and loss of identity. A sense of menace pervades many of the stories as well as a dark humour. Others are heart-breaking. Nod Ghosh writes with masterful control and insight and it is the power of what she has left unstated, as well as her eloquent use of language that pierces the heart. *Filthy Sucre* is a compelling and sometimes painful evocation of what can happen to the human spirit. These are stories that resonate in the mind and the heart long after the book is closed.

~ Sandra Arnold, author of *The Ash, the Well and the Bluebell* and *Soul Etchings*

The three novellas in *Filthy Sucre* are utterly gripping, to the point that they become addictive. Nod Ghosh combines solid characterisation with fast-paced storytelling and beautiful prose, three ingredients that make it impossible for the reader to put this book down.

~ Sophie van Llewyn, author of *Bottled Goods*

filthy sucre

THREE NOVELLAS

Nod Ghosh

TRUTH SERUM PRESS

TRUTH SERUM PRESS

Filthy Sucre copyright © Nod Ghosh
First published as a book February 2020 by Truth Serum Press

BP#00086

ISBN: 978-1-925536-92-8

Truth Serum Press
32 Meredith Street
Sefton Park SA 5083
Australia

Email: truthserumpress@live.com.au
Website: https://truthserumpress.net
Truth Serum Press catalogue: https://truthserumpress.net/catalogue/

Also available as an eBook
ISBN: 978-1-925536-93-5

Original cover photographs:
Franz Josef Glacier original photo and adaptation copyright © Nod Ghosh
Milky way starry sky night sky star copyright © FelixMittermeier
Cover design copyright © Matt Potter
Author photograph used by permission of the author

Truth Serum Press is a member of the
Bequem Publishing collective
http://www.bequempublishing.com/

To all the bad arses out there.

I'd say you know who you are,
but you probably don't.

Sugar in the Folds, Sand in the Creases

Sugar in the Dirt

Every time I come on this cliff top walk, I remember the very last time I came here with you.

You drove me in your clapped out old Ford. The wind howled that afternoon. You parked next to a wreck with a flat tyre, the only other car around. I was wearing a pair of high-heeled sling backs. You walked faster than me, and I had to run in short spurts to keep up with you. I wore a lock of your hair in a pendant around my neck. I wore a chip of stone in my heart.

"Where are we going, Vincent?" I'd asked.

"You'll see."

I would have followed you anywhere. You'd planted something deep inside me, and then erased it with your callous indifference.

I knew it was the end.

I felt sick, asked if we could stop a while, but you made me walk on regardless. We entered the gloom under a canopy of trees. I stumbled on leaves and ashy loam, a carpet of death and decay, strewn thickly like discarded body parts. Their browning marked the impermanence of all things fresh, all things wholesome. I stumbled on my words.

"S — slow down."

"We're almost there." You stopped between two evergreens and peered into the gloom beneath the trees. I put my hand on your shoulder, and you turned around.

"Tania, I've something to tell you."

It wasn't your words, it was the way you said them, the way you retracted from my touch.

"It's her," I said, "the girl from the record store, isn't it?"

You didn't flinch. "Her name is Elina."

"Why her? What's so special about — " The words grated in my throat as I spoke. Questioning was useless.

3

"It's just — "

You left it at that and strode on two paces ahead of me. I followed, and wondered why you'd brought me to this particular spot. Veering towards a clearing on the left, you stopped and I nearly walked into you.

"This is where Elina and I first made love," you said. *Made love?* Was that really you talking, Vincent? You pointed to a clearing between the trees, a spot secluded enough to passers by, but public enough to appeal to your sense of riskiness, the thrill of being caught. Almost. You'd wanted me to catch you, leaving enough clues, but not too many.

"Why are you telling me this?"

"I want you to understand, Tania."

"What if I don't want to?" I said through gritted teeth.

"I know you will."

And even as you described how you'd lain in the sandy soil and undone her buttons, I knew you were right. I *would* want to know every move, every penetrating detail, everything that spelled the end of us. I knew, even as you described the sand in the creases of her skin, the softness of her tongue, I'd ask you again and again to tell me exactly what you'd done, and how you'd done it, as if telling me would exorcise Elina from your mind, like the others before her.

I knew as you described the sugar in the folds of her lips that this would be the last departure.

Sugar Turns Sour

I think I am the winner when you bring record to me at counter. Record by bands named *Spirit, Meat Cleaver,* and *Acid Spot.* I am liking your smile from first time I see you. You wipe something from my face when you pay. You almost touch my lip. You write your name and telephone number, so I can call when new album is come. V-I-N-C-E-N-T.

"Unusual name," you say, your eyes on my nametag. "Elina. Exotic." You say it like you are sipping a fine wine. Your eyes move to place between my neck and work blouse.

"You're not from around here, are you?"

"I am here one year. Then go back," I say. "But to stay here. This I want."

A girl come to counter and pull your hand. "Let's go," she say. Her feet are like falukorv sausage, swollen through strap of her high-heeled shoes. "We need to go."

She is, how you say? Unhappy? Mistempered?

"Now," she say.

"Give it a rest, Tania," you say. "I'm coming." She pull you. She pull your eye from me.

I am not liking this Tania. She is not liking me.

The next day you come without her.

"Can I help?" Old Timmins asks, but you shake head. No. When my boss goes to stockroom, you lean over counter.

"Do you have anything by a band," you say, "a very special band." You are whispering. "It's called, *I can't stop thinking about you?*"

"Really? That is band?"

"Yes," you say, but your smile gives a different answer.

"I check on catalogue?" My smile too has message for you.

"Sure," you say, "or you could come by my place later and I could let you hear some of their work. I think you'd like it. I really do."

5

"That, I would like."

"What time do you finish, Elina? I'll pick you up."

And this is how it begins.

Of course there is no band. Of course you don't take me home. Maybe she is there, the woman, this Tania. We go instead to a place. How you say? The cliff top walk. You take me between trees, where no one is seeing. You tell my face is like sugar.

"Sugar, Sugar," you say, and I know I have you now. Not this Tania.

This is where we are first in love. In sandy soil.

I have you now. I am winner. Not Tania.

You forgot our anniversary, Vincent, and then you kiss another woman. I saw you in the dim light of the Ala Roma tavern. You did not see me. I had driven to liquor store to buy bourbon for you. Then I saw you in Ala Roma booth, and my breath was gone.

I threw your gift on the floor at your feet when you came home.

"This is for five years of marriage you miserable pig. *Skitstövel.*"

You denied everything, as you held my wrists in your hands, but I knew. I saw it. She was, how do you say, a tramp? Her hair in a bun, all fancy, but never the less, a tramp. I recognised this tramp. She'd served coffee and doughnuts to us at Charlie's café, pulling her short, short skirt up her thick, thick thighs, purring like a lioness when she fetched your café mocha.

"I don't know what you're talking about Elina," you said. But after five years, my lips are no longer sugar to yours.

I am crushed by the bitterness of your lies.

I thought I was the winner.

But now, I am not so certain.

The Poisonous Touch of Sugar

You don't do a thing for the kids. I can't understand why you don't at least clean up after yourself, Vince. And if I say anything, it's me, *me* who's at fault.

I've taken it for nearly ten years now. I tried. I really tried to get through to you yesterday.

All you said was, "Stop moaning, woman."

"But – "

"I'm going out, Sheryl."

Bang. And you were gone.

I dropped Misty, Callie and Red at school and did the weekly shop. I carried everything home in a shopping trolley, because you drove the Cavalier to work, even though you could've taken the bus. I told Misty to take the trolley back, so I could reclaim the coin. She asked if she could keep it, so I gave her 20p. I couldn't spare it, but I gave it to her anyway.

Yesterday wasn't the first time you stayed out all night. You've done that plenty of times after we've fought. I don't know what I would have done if you'd come back. I wanted to tear you to shreds. And I wanted you with a hunger so great, it hollowed me out, Vince.

Last night, I hugged your pillow to my chest. I remembered a time when your scent affected me so deeply I couldn't eat, sleep or keep my shit together.

I couldn't sleep last night. So I got out of bed and wrecked your stuff.

"Where's Daddy?" Red asks. I'm making porridge and he winds around my legs.

"Work," I lie.

"But it's the weekend," Callie says. "Daddy's coming to see me at football, isn't he?"

"What's this?" Red picks up a shard of vinyl.

"Something happened to Daddy's big C.D.s." Misty has a piece of your *Spirit* album cover in her hands.

Red creeps around her feet, picking at parts of the broken disc.

"Look Mummy," Misty says. "There's more. Who made all this mess? Have we been robbed?"

Callie's face crumples. Her lips draw down at the corners and her shoulders shake.

"Oh honey," I say, as Callie starts to cry.

Mum and Brad collect the kids and take them to Callie's football match. I need to be at Franklyn's bistro for ten. My hair looks good in a bun. I've dressed carefully, enough to make an impression, but not gone too far. I really need this job. They're not hiring at Charlie's right now, though Charlie said he'd take me on again if he could. I've bills to pay. I owe Geordie next-door twenty quid. Misty needs new shoes.

I walk into Franklyn's and choke back a cry. You have your back to me. I return to the entrance lobby, though I can still hear you. Peeping through the wall of coats, I wait. Your ex-wife's hand is in yours. The bistro is noisy, but I pick out some of what you say.

"Sugar," your voice is soft, coaxing, but I can hear you all the same.

"When?" she asks. She says more, but I don't catch her words.

"Soon," you say. "It's . . . it's got to be done right, Elina."

She screws her face up. I don't hear what she says. She pulls her hand up and draws a finger across her pretty neck. I used to be jealous of your ex-wife's looks. Tall. Blonde. I used to look dumpy next to her.

Right now she looks like she's sucking a sour plum.

You squeeze her hand.

"I need to get Sheryl – " I jump at the sound of my name, and strain to hear what you say. But your voice is swallowed by the clang of cutlery and the whoosh of the coffee machine. " – need to do it right."

" – when she is gone – " She taps her long nail on the table.

"She'll be gone soon, Sugar. Soon."

I walk out of the bistro.

Seems you have plans for me I wasn't counting on.

8

But Then There's Always Sarah

Shit your life is a mess, mate. You look like you're half way to hell.

Still, get a shave, motherfucker, before they're all in here splashing, squirting toothpaste, and screeching like rabid monkeys. Where's your razor? Ouch! What the? Red's Lego is everywhere. Arsehole. Why can't Sheryl keep this place clean? And the kids have got chalk all over the carpet. You pick up a half-crushed piece and put it in your pocket.

Mess.

Mess.

Mess.

How did things become so complicated?

You came back last night, and Sheryl said nothing about your fight. Nah. Had to be something wrong. She was all *here's your dinner*, and *go kiss the girls goodnight*, while the T.V. screamed something about terrorists. And the kids were bleating in your ear. *Daddy you missed my football match*, and Misty said something about your records being broken. What records? You've never broken a record in your life. Never been good enough. Fast enough. Clever enough. Slow, stupid Vince.

Thought you were so clever climbing into bed with Sheryl. But she pulled away from you, so you had to spit in your hand and use that instead.

Mess.

You walk downstairs in the morning. There's carnage every-where. The house is a tip. Looks like shit in the grey light. She forgot to take out the rubbish.

Your ex-wife thinks you're going to leave Sheryl and get back with her.

No.

Fuckin'.

Way.

Elina's not right in the head. Still, if you want to cut the payments, you'll have to think outside the − hey, where are your fuckin' boots? Where's −?

What's going on? And what's that in the corner with Callie's football gear? Shit, it's your *Meat Cleaver* album − what's left of it!

"Sheryl?" She's not in bed. "Sheryl? Where's my jacket? Where's my − "

A small face appears at the doorway. That familiar intake of breath followed by a mewling wail. Callie's crying again.

You step outside. Sheryl's standing next to the Cav with some guy. His arms look like they're made from wood. He rolls his hands into fists. What the?

"I want you gone, Vincent," he says, his voice like cardboard.

"Sheryl ... Sugar?"

"Don't call me Sugar."

"Who the fuck's this? What's he doin' in my − "

You don't wait for a reply as his fist flies towards your face.

Run.

Run.

Run.

When life gets this crazy, there's always Sarah. But Sarah's not been opening her door to you. You bang on the wood. Ta-rat-a-tat-tat. You know she's there from the shadows shifting in the window. You shout her name until you're hoarse. You're about to turn away. Where to? Fuck knows. Try again.

"Sarah!"

Is that a *guy* in there? Suck in your breath. Hands in pockets. What's that? Some other prick's not stepping in on your patch. So you take the chalk from your pocket and write on the pavement.

S-A-R-A-H

Big fat letters.

I LOVE YOU.

Big fat lies.

Dancing with Wings

So many years have passed. I have not seen my family since before I married you, Vincent. They missed our wedding. They missed our divorce. Too difficult for them to come, and I have not returned home. The flights aren't cheap. I am so busy with work, and my mother does not trust the planes anymore, thinks they will fall out of the sky. But now I am here, I know there is another reason I have stayed away. I have not seen Aunt Mariana since I left this place. I have not wanted to.

So often I talked to my mother on the telephone and on the Skype, while you were out doing things with cars and other women.

I saw my sister's children on the screen, babies then toddlers. There was a hollowness in my belly. The children danced, shouting and laughing. We did not know if the barrenness was from my womb or your seed, until that waitress from Charlie's café presented you with her child.

Slut.

My sister's children danced with wings.

Children changed to teenagers as the years passed, and the hollowness did not go.

"Elina," my mother said when I called a month ago, "I am an old lady." It was good to hear her voice, the lilt of my own language. Not so good to hear what she said. "I will die soon. When you will come?"

"Ma, you always say this." It was true. Even when we were first married, so many years ago, she was saying such a thing. She always asked me to come home, but for many years, I ignored. Then Aunt Mariana came onto the screen, her words held a knife to my throat. *It's different this time*, my aunt said. *Cancer.* I thought of how I would feel if I never saw my mother again. *Deep inside her and through all of her*, my aunt continued. *It will kill her within months. You will come?*

It wasn't really a question. My mouth showed as a straight line on

11

one corner of the screen, but I obeyed Mariana, just as I always had.

"I'll come."

Now my mother's hand is in mine, her skin is the colour of turmeric. My sister's children open the gifts I have brought, and thank me in perfect English. I twist the ring I've started to wear again. Your ring. It leaves faint green marks on my skin, like it always used to. I find comfort in those green stains.

Mariana is here. She asks about you. She asks if I have any boyfriend. I think of telling there is Erik in my life, but I don't. It is like I do you a disservice. Your love has caramelised inside me, and all the Eriks and Raymonds and Alberts and Wallaces cannot crack through its brittle shell. I wish you were here, Vincent. There is hunger in my aunt's eyes. It scares me. Aunt Mariana walks across my mother's parlour and takes my hand, and a knot of fear grips my stomach. I want to escape her, but I cannot. She pulls away after a while.

Lina, the youngest niece jumps onto my lap. There is a tremble in my thigh, and the small girl jiggles with excitement, and I remember.

I am seven.

My Aunt has come to visit. There are presents in her bag, and starlight in her eyes. I adore her. My sister and I compete for her attention, but I know it is me she loves most, because she told me. We dance in the parlour, and when Mariana lifts me in her arms, I am so close to flying, so very close, I could burst.

Later, in the darkness of our bedroom, my sister and I sleep, curled together like crawling vines. The door clicks, and a shaft of light cuts across the room. I am tense like a spring. I know what is to happen, because it has happened before. My sister sleeps beside me, her breath heavy. The door closes. A hand reaches under the covers.

This is what it means to love. This is the true meaning of flight. Not even you, Vincent, can make me fly in this way.

This is the dance that never ends.

Buried in Your Kisses

You tried to come back into my life Vincent, but I wouldn't let you. I couldn't. There's a stronger force beside me now, and he won't let me come to you. I heard you bang on the wood of my door. Ta-rat-a-tat-tat. You called my name. But I didn't answer.

"Leave it, Sarah," he'd said, "the guys a loser." I shrank under the strength of his arm.

He was right.

He pulled me away from the window and kissed me, and I wanted to taste the blood-heat of your lips, feel the hurt of your love.

I feel wretched when you hold me, Vincent, but it makes me whole.

You fix the brokenness inside me.

I heard you shout, while he pulled the covers over us and entered me without a word. I longed for the intensity of your loving.

We were going nowhere, you and I. I know we never will. Your children, your complexity, the other women in your life.

But still.

I love it when you whisper *sugar* in my ear. I long for the limitlessness of your loving, as wide as the sea.

It's a blustery morning. The windows rattle in their frames. He left an hour ago, and then rang from the office, told me not to open the door to anyone. It was another of his unwanted gifts. His caring. His overwrought protectiveness. I phone back to check he's there, and let my breath escape in semi-quavers. I change channels on the television, but they all say the same thing.

Outside, I see the letters of my name scratched into the pavement, partly washed away by rain and the scuff of his boots.

*

All I can think of is how you want me back, how you love me, and the pain of never being buried in your kisses again is enough to kill me, cell by cell. He has deleted your number from my phone, but I know it off by heart.

You answer after four rings.

I could die right now, and I would be happy.

Your words are liquid gold in my ear.

Ignoble Metal

Through the night, a dream of metal cuts through your skin, so you wake up screaming. There is no one here to comfort you, no one who gives a damn.

In the communal bathroom, you wipe a patch of steam off the glass, and stare at your drawn face. You've lost weight, pal. You hold your hand up to your chin. The ring glints like a lie.

You wore the wedding band to meet Elina at Franklyn's. It's been on ever since.

Why?

The fourth finger of your left hand burns. You want to cut the finger off. Cut all traces of your ex-wife away. But you know you can't.

You didn't sleep well. The shower spurts alternate hot and cold streams, and you don't want to spend too long in there. There's thick black mould around the showerhead. It comes away on your thumb. When you get out, you almost shout to Sheryl for a towel. But Sheryl's not there. Shit. It's just you now. You slip your T-shirt and boxers on over wet skin.

That old guy from the end room is in the corridor. Albert. Albert Timmins. They say he used to be a doctor or a priest or a lawyer until something happened to his brain. He groans and pulls a piece of chewing gum from behind his ear and slips it into his mouth. You walk past trying not to catch his eye, but he captures you with a look, as if he's casting a blessing over you.

Back in your room, you try to forget the old man. You remove the ring. It takes a while. You're thinner than you were, but not as slim as when you married Elina. You wrap the glinting circle in a page of the *Evening Post* and slide it into one of the cardboard boxes on the floor. You wonder if you'd ever be able to find it again. There's no definite place for anything in the rough room of the hostel. There's no definite place for you in the world.

The newspaper on the floor has six-inch-high headlines about nothing in particular. It's two weeks old, but you read it for something to do.

You'll probably not care if you never find the wedding ring again, though it could be worth a quid or two. You wonder if Elina still has hers. You wonder if she ever discovered it wasn't really gold.

You think about a woman you once knew. You wonder what Tania Carter is doing now.

Tania used to buy herself jewellery and gift-wrap it so you could give it to her.

When she bought herself a diamond solitaire, you left.

On the Road Again

I pick up petrol and burgers for the kids, and have six quid left. Your old Cavalier smells like a hot iron. Something's going to fall apart, but I keep driving. Away from my mother. Away from her husband. Away from our home. Away from you, Vince.

My mum's never done that before. Never told us we weren't welcome. Brad was standing right behind her, like she was a robot, and he was operating controls on her back.

"You can't stay here, Sheryl."

She'd ruffled the hair on Red's head, when he tried to push past her. Brad pressed another button, and she shoved her grandson away, back towards me. "You'd better go now. You've — "

"We're not staying." I'd grabbed Red's hand, hadn't stopped to listen to her accusations and lies. Misty had whined about having left something-or-other at her grandmother's, but I barked an order and forced her into the car. Bang. A corner of her dress flapped through the door, but I left it there.

Trapped.

"Where are we going, Mum?" Callie moans. Misty asks for the third time if she can open the door.

"My dress is stuck. I can't move."

"Will we see Daddy?" Red asks.

You never have to deal with any of this, do you, Vince? You never did.

"Daddy won't see you," I lie. "He doesn't want to." That's when I bite back a tear. Remember how you pounded at the door, your voice hoarse, Red straining on the other side to get to you. But Nat wasn't going to let you near us. I'd given him a look that said *just this once?* I'd pleaded with my eyes. I'd pay the price for that later. Nat's not the sort of man to cross. Even if you only do it with your eyes.

There's a whimpering sound above the whirr of the engine. Callie's crying again.

Franklyn paid me fair and square for the shifts I'd done at the bistro, and a little extra because he cared.

"I can't keep you on, Sheryl," he'd said. "You're a good waitress, but I need someone I can count on."

What am I supposed to do? I can't leave the kids at home by themselves. And I sure as hell wasn't going to let *you* anywhere near them.

"Where are we going, Mum?" Callie asks for the thousandth time.

"Somewhere full of sunshine and unicorns, honey."

The road ahead turns glassy in a heat-haze. We may have nothing but the clothes on our backs, but we're together. And we're going away from all of this. We're going somewhere you'll never find us.

Misty

Mumma said I couldn't take all my toys. Said I wouldn't need them where we were going. And I didn't pack any clothes. Didn't have enough time. We left Grandma's almost as soon as we got there.

We got burgers though. I had chips with mine. And sauce. Mumma never got one, and that made me sad, how she always does things for us, but not for herself. When we got going again, Red was shouting like the world was on fire.

"Faster Mum, go faster."

So she did. There was a smell that wasn't there before, like something hot and blistered. I was scared.

"I'm gonna play you each a song. A special song," Mumma said, and the whine of the go-faster pedal screamed big and loud. The Cavalier veered in and out of the fast lane as she twisted dials and pressed buttons. Red had his song first. He sang along to the words he knew.

— *a handsome man* —

He laughed like a hyena when the chorus came on, like he always did.

Mum went a little faster. I thought she might get a ticket, but there weren't so many cars on the motorway by then. A little slip of moon climbed into the corner of the candy-pink sky, but the air blowing through my window was hot and steamy.

Callie starts to cry when her song comes on.

"Where are we going, Mum?" she moans over the words and music.

"Listen to your song, honey," Mumma says. I feel like crying along with my sister. My dress is caught in the car door, and Mumma won't stop so I can't release it. I've left my bag at Grandma's, and it's got all my make-up in it. And my trading cards.

"My dress is stuck. I can't move," I say again.

"Are we going to see Daddy?" Red asks.

Callie asks Mumma where we're going again.

"Somewhere you can see unicorns prancing, where you sleep on candyfloss pillows."

I don't believe her.

"Your turn now, Misty," Mumma says. There's a catch in her voice, like she's trying not to cry.

But then my song comes on and the tangle inside my chest loosens a bit. It's something Grandma used to play for Mumma when she was little. Whenever I hear it, I feel light. Like marshmallow.

— *in love again* —

My song makes me think of sherbet and sugar. It makes me think of being in love, even though I never have been. It makes me feel like there're little bits of God even in forgotten corners.

And though I didn't think the Cavalier could go any faster, somehow it does.

It's flying.

Come Away With Me

You tried to come back into my life Vincent, but I wouldn't let you. He wouldn't let me let you. But your strength lies in your tenacity.

When he was at work one day, you slipped back in, between the folds. We took his diamond cuff links, and a little cash. On the bus north, you waited until dark, then took my hand and slid it into places you shouldn't. We wanted to go somewhere no one could find us. I've never been this far north before.

The grey blanket of dawn is heavy on my shoulders, and I am tired when we arrive. Oh so tired, but giddy with joy at the thought of being with you. Inebriated. We have enough money for the smallest room on the top floor of a dingy motel, a dirty grey building with tiny windows. I pay for two nights.

"Sarah," you whisper, and close my eyes with kisses. "Sarah, Sugar." The blinds are drawn against the gelatinous sky that threatens to burst with snow, while we burst with longing.

The way you hold me makes me whole. I am broken inside. Only you can fix me, only you, my love. I am sore from your loving. Splinters of pain break from my newest bruises. You rub me until all that is left is a stain. I am washed away in a tide of kisses.

I love it when you whisper in my ear.

Snow falls silently. The insane luminosity of it takes everything else away.

The Scent of Metal

He calls the day after I fly back from seeing my mother.

"The name's Brad Freeman," he says. His voice is grit and bone. Is it an angriness? I do not know this man.

"Is that Elina?" he asks.

"Yes. I am Elina." It's late, very late for this. I think I should end the telephone call from this crazy who is called Brad — Brad, I cannot remember the surname. "What is it you want?"

"It's about your ex-husband." He speaks your name, and a wave of fear cuts through my body. Something has happened to you? Is that why you did not call when I was at my mother's?

"Yes?" I wait for him to speak. There is a taste in my mouth. It reminds me of the tang of brass. "He is all right?" I think of the metal ornaments my Aunt Mariana gave me, shining animals I would suck when frightened to have their brassy tingle comfort my tongue.

"We need to find him." The man pauses. "Any idea where he might be?" Relief floods through me, but the metallic taste stays in my mouth. I can smell it when I breathe, like metal filings in the air. I have not heard from you for over a week. You should have called by now. But this man is trying to find you. Perhaps you hide somewhere?

"He is all right?" I ask the man again. Maybe you have done something. Something dangerous. Maybe this Brad, he is police. "Where you are calling from?" I ask.

"It's about Sheryl." His strident voice cuts into me, like he can wound me with her name. The bitch from Charlie's café. It wasn't enough that you fucked her. You filled her belly with children and left me. The taste in the air becomes a molten ball that sinks to the emptiness in my abdomen. I want you back, Vincent, no matter what you have done.

"She is — she is?" I cannot say. What have you done, my love? I cannot make the words. So I wait for him to speak.

"Sheryl is my — I'm Sheryl's stepfather. We need to find your ex-husband." Again there is angriness in the man's voice. "We think you know where he is."

What have you done? Your whore's stepfather thinks I will give you away. Can this man know about us? Did you tell anyone you were coming back to me? Back to your wife as you should.

You'd said yourself it was too soon to tell anyone.

"I have no idea where he is," I tell this man Brad. "I don't see him." The metallic smell becomes stronger as I spin the lie. The half-lie. It becomes a cord around my throat, choking me. "Do not call this number again."

"Elina. Please. There's been an — we need to talk to him. It's — it's an emergency."

I hesitate for one second before disconnecting. Perhaps it is your children who need you. What have you done? Did you get rid of our little problem? Did you do something to their mother?

But I cannot help him, this man called Brad. I cannot help, because like him, I have no clue where you are.

The smell is so strong now, forging a memory of this moment under my skin. Yet I know the odour is only in my mind. When I cut the man's voice off, I cannot know that this moment, this day, will change everything between us, Vincent.

I want the metallic tang to disappear. It cuts into my brain and carves a piece of me away.

But the smell only grows stronger.

Callie-Blue

When I wake up, you're sitting beside me, Daddy, and all the pain goes away — for a minute, but then I remember the other pain, and it starts all over again.

You wipe my tears with your handkerchief. Then you take out your cigarettes, and light one up. I love that smell. I love that I'm taking in the same air that you've been breathing. For a minute it feels like everything is good, and I am safe again. But then Mary-Jane appears and tells you off.

"You can't smoke in here, sir." She stiffens, and the hairs on her top lip wobble when she makes her mouth into a line. "Dr. Timmins doesn't allow smoking on the ward." She says his name, *Dr. Timmins*, like he's some sort of God.

Fuck him.

"I'll see you in a minute, Callie," you say, and my hand slips from yours.

"But you only just got here, Daddy — "

You're gone before I finish speaking. I hold the tears in. You'll be back. I wanted you so much when you weren't here, Daddy. And every time I asked for you, Mary-Jane said they'd find you soon.

I knew I couldn't ask for Mumma.

I begin to count my breaths. I try to remember how long it takes to smoke a cigarette, so I know when you'll be back. And I count. And I count.

I always wanted a colour for a name.

I'm still counting.

When my brother was born, you called him Red. I wanted a new name so badly when he arrived, and I wasn't the baby anymore.

I count for a little bit longer.

Mumma called me Callie-Blue for a while after Red was born. But she was busy with the baby and everything, and she soon forgot.

And I'm still counting.

Maid of the Mist

Erik lowers himself to his knees when we approach the Bridal Veil Falls, and I wonder if the arthritis is bad for him.

"Elina," he says, and I know in an instant, I have made a mistake coming away on holiday with this man. With this, how you say, this boyfriend. Can you call a fifty-nine-year-old man a boy?

I too, am not in the springtime of youth, but part of me is young. I must act now, as I should have done days, weeks, months ago.

I don't want this man. I want you, Vincent, now you are free. Free now, because your whore has died.

I could have said I wouldn't come with this man, this Erik. But you didn't call for so many days. I couldn't think of a reason why I shouldn't have this trip. I've always wanted to come here.

And now. And now I hear you are back. Returned, but speechless with grief.

They found you somewhere in Scotland. What were you doing there?

Erik reaches under the blue rain-cape, water droplets catching on his pale eyelashes. He's looking for something. I cannot wash away the thoughts of you. The idiot has raised one knee. Why did you not call me? I must do what I can to stop this man.

"Erik," I say. I fill the word with meaning.

"Yes, Elina." His eyes mist over, "I – "

"Erik." I am firmer this time. I say his name, but the way I say it has a hundred other meanings. And all of them say STOP. STOP NOW. This is my meaning.

He hesitates, fiddles with the cape. The tour guide looks over, as if expecting a sign. Oh Holy God. The fool has spoken to someone else of this?

"Elina, I want – "

"Erik, we have to talk."

He makes a sound.

25

"Now," I say.

And as I cut this man down, break him into pieces, rebuff his offer before he has made it, I remember when you proposed to me, Vincent.

I look away from Erik, look away from the tour guide, look away from the cluster of blue-caped people, cameras poised.

You took me to the trees near the cliff top walk that day. You took me back to where we first made love. You laid me down on a blanket of leaves. You took my hand. You made me a happiest woman.

Afterwards, we talked of future. We talked of where to live. We talked of making children.

But children never came.

Until now.

The spray from the falls makes my face wet.

This man, Erik, has walked away into a confusion of blue capes.

It is then that I feel a flutter, like wings in my belly. My little Röd. Our little Röd, for I know he is a boy.

To lose one son and gain another.

This is my gift to you, my love.

I know the child in my belly is yours.

Her Small Hand

Her small hand squeezes yours.

"I miss Red and Misty," she says, and stifles a sniffle. "I miss Mumma too," her voice almost a whisper. You savour every movement of her fingers, not knowing how well the rest of her broken body will move when the recovery is complete.

You weren't here when it happened. But they found you. Found you to tell you two of your children were gone.

You came back with a woman who wouldn't stop crying, and you wanted to tell her to shut up.

"It's not like it happened to you, Sarah," is all you said. But she kept on crying. She tried to hold your hand, but you wouldn't let her. The woman gave you all she could. But you have nothing left to give her.

After you get back from the hospital, your ex-wife calls, and it's the same thing all over again. Do they think smothering you with sympathy will make a difference? Do they think it'll make you *like* them more?

"Elina, I can't talk right now," you say.

"But Vincent, I must tell you something," she says.

She choses this moment to tell you she's pregnant. Says it's your child.

"You sure it's mine? We only – " You sigh. "And what about that old guy you're seeing?" Your voice fades to a hiss. "If that bastard can still get it up." You're angry. So angry. Does she think this will make you like her?

Returning to the hospital, her small hand stirs in yours. And then she starts to cry.

Teeth

I don't know why I thought of you today, Vincent. I don't often dwell on ex-boyfriends. I haven't seen you for decades.

I rarely walk through the trees near the cliff top. The mumbling autumn leaves and pervasive loamy smell remind me of the very last time we came here. You drove me in that rusty brown Ford of yours.

You said, *Tania, I have something to tell you.*

I used to think about you constantly. I couldn't stop. But the blood in my veins froze when you told me you were leaving.

I could have killed you. Or her. That bitch you left me for who could hardly string a sentence together without murdering the language.

I rarely think of you these days, unless I'm walking along this path. Occasionally I catch the scent of you in other places. It must be my imagination, but your essence triggers memories. You used to tell me I was beautiful. You said we'd be together forever. You'd call me every sweet name known to man. I think of you when I run the gold chain I bought through my fingers. I wanted something from you on my birthday, so I made you give it to me.

Sugar.

The locket still has your hair in it. Matted and tattered, it has the look of something partially consumed. I tried to sell it once, the locket, not the hair. But gold isn't worth what it once was. There was a time I thought my mouth held a fortune, with all the gold fillings I had. Could've done with the cash if anyone had wanted them.

Not long after I tried to sell the locket all my teeth fell out. I don't know why. Maybe my bones couldn't hold onto them anymore. It's hard to keep hold of everything. Perhaps I didn't look after them well enough, though I don't often crave sweet things. I despise the texture of sugar on my tongue. Even the sound of the word makes me sick.

Some poisons settle in the folds and creases of the mind and stay there forever. You, Vincent, were my poison, but I am stronger now. I can see you for what you were. I don't need you anymore.

Another Silent Movie

Damien

Roland has fallen in love with a boy on the bus.

They ride the top deck on Monday. This boy sits at the front surrounded by others in maroon College School uniforms. The College School girls have smoky eyes and drip jewellery. The boys have defaced their blazer badges and sewn triangular flares into their trousers. Their make-up is more Bowie than Bolan, crafted with eye shadow stolen from their girlfriends and mothers.

Roland sits near the steps with the silent Grammar School boys.

His face is cosmetic free and clean-shaven, slapped pink by the cold.

The boy he loves looks older than Roland. He's taller, with broader shoulders.

When he cracks a joke, the floor detonates with laughter. The boy turns to face his audience, their smiles and rejoinders captured in his slate-grey eyes. In a flurry of mock self-aggrandisement, the boy takes a bow and thanks them. His tones are gravel and cream.

They cross the motorway bridge.

Red sunglow slices through the bus window and highlights dandelion hairs on the boy's cheek. He's at the cusp of puberty, the dawn of adulthood.

When the boy stands to leave the bus, Roland senses the patchouli scent of sweat. The boy's limbs are long and muscled. His wheat-coloured hair swings when he twists down the steps.

The bus pulls into the stop at the Charnwood estate. This is where the rough kids live according to Roland's mother, though he doesn't always believe what she says.

Roland doesn't travel on the bus every day, only when his mother cannot collect him from school. She frowns when she counts out coins for his fare on Tuesday morning.

"Sorry, I have another meeting tonight." Her voice is lambs' wool apologetic, so different from the cardboard of the night before. She'd read his homework book with the hunger of an inquisitor. She'd taken in the 'B minus' grades with their *could do better* innuendo. Roland had braced himself for violence.

He escaped without bruises on this occasion.

Roland doesn't care that she can't collect him after school, though he must pretend he does. He looks forward to the days she works late.

On Tuesday afternoon, the College School boy struts up the metal steps, his blazer slung over one shoulder. His stance is lion-assured. He takes his usual seat.

"Damien!" A girl insinuates her way next to the boy. She leans into his body. Silver-white hair falls around her Mary Quant face.

Damien gesticulates to the girl, mimes serving her a dish, impersonating a waiter from something on television. The girl's laughter infects the maroon uniformed kids. Roland sees the boy dip forward and kiss the girl's hand. When he comes up again, his features are contorted. He's squeaks like a rat, and pokes her in the ribs.

"Don't!" the girl screams, though the way she leans into him suggests she would hate it if he stopped.

Roland burns.

The Grammar School boys don't speak to the College School kids. They barely speak to one another. These bright boys twist anxious hands into knots as ruby-skies roll past. These future leaders ignore graffiti on the seats in front of them. Their eyes skim back and forth, left to right. They don't want to know who loves whom. They don't care whether *Yes* are better than *Aerosmith*. These young prodigies don't want to read football chants punctuated by gum.

The Grammar School boys stare in silence, as if it is their birthright to be bored.

The College School pupils smoke and swear. The driver with *Twilight Zone* eyes tolerates their indiscretions, but his shoulders ease when several alight at the Charnwood estate.

*

On Wednesday afternoon, Roland sits a little further forward. It's the last day of term. Only five College School kids board at the concrete building. Damien looks around at the top of the stairs and chooses the seat in front of Roland. When he turns, the boy's smile is cotton wool and glitter stars. He flicks open a box of cigarettes.

"Want one?"

The aroma reminds Roland of his father. The air is heavy with rain-clouds and anticipation. The metallic rush of possibility is intoxicating.

Roland returns the smile. A primordial fire ignites inside him. He takes the smoke and leans forward. The boy cups his hand around the flame and lights Roland's cigarette.

Morley Lane

"Keep the door locked when I'm out," Roland's mother bleats.

"I might run to the shops for a snack," he replies.

"It's not safe for youngsters to go out on their own," she says. "Especially these days."

Youngsters.

"I've got a real urge for smoky bacon crisps," he says, though food is the last thing on his mind.

"You can have a biscuit if you're hungry," she snaps. "It's been getting dark around half four." She folds her grey pac-a-mac into the shopping basket. "And there's that man in a raincoat who does dirty things," she adds. "I heard about him on the radio."

She's always hearing things on the radio, Roland says to the Nicotiana sylvestris plants, his mother's pride and joy. He's in the corridor, out of earshot.

She can't keep him imprisoned forever. Roland's mother is only there because she's taken Thursday afternoon off work. She's vacuumed the whole house. Everything's got to be spick and span before her party at the weekend. Roland has had the house to himself all morning. It's been intoxicating. His mother's office closes next week for Christmas, but until then — who knows what might happen when she's at work and he's off school?

Roland waits in his room.

Listening to forty-fives, he keeps the volume low, so he'll know when she leaves the house. Surely she can't watch him every second of the day.

Roland waits.

He knows the College School kids from the bus will meet at the pond at the abandoned quarry this afternoon. He knows they'll have music. Maybe they'll smoke some pot. Perhaps some of the couples will make out.

He knows they won't stay long. There's a chance of frost later on.

Roland's mother pops her head into his room. "I'm going now. Was it cheese and onion flavour you wanted?"

"Smoky bacon," he says.

She's humming *Angels from the Realms of Glory*. She must be in a good mood.

"Please," he adds, so as not to dispel the good cheer.

"I'm buying Gruyère cheese and kirsch for fondue," she says. "Mince pies too. And fruit." She has the wicker gondola basket with her, the one she carries her fruit in. "I'll be out for two hours. Maybe more." She likes to examine her oranges and pick them carefully.

"Don't rush. You know how the shops are crammed at this time of year." He tries to sound solicitous. "Take your time."

"Yes, but remember to keep the door locked. And don't answer the telephone," she adds, blowing him a kiss. He'll obey her commands.

What his mother doesn't know is that her son will be on the wrong side of that locked door.

Roland waits until the crunch of tyres on gravel tells him his mother has pulled her car out of the garage.

Damien, the blonde-haired boy from the bus, has told Roland where the College School kids meet. Damien wants him there. Roland knows this because he wouldn't have given him the time, the place, and told him about the risk of getting caught, if he hadn't meant it.

He knows Damien likes him. He'd laughed at Roland's jokes and given him that rosebud smile.

A minute after his mother leaves, Roland locks the door behind him. He steps into the street as her Cortina turns away at the bottom of the hill. Looking down at his feet, he curses. His plimsolls, shiny anorak and unbranded straight-leg jeans are an embarrassment. Levis cost too much, according to his mother.

The wind whips the languid grass into knots. Bracken cracks underfoot, brittle and dry. He smells wood smoke, but no one's arrived yet. The water glints in the low sun. For one second, Roland wonders whether Damien has been playing games with him. Maybe the College School kids are meeting somewhere warm and dry, laughing about the square Grammar School boy waiting in the cold, in his shiny anorak.

He walks to the pathway that skirts a cliff face and leads to the top of the rocks that provide a backdrop for the violet water.

Roland is out of breath from the climb. He sits at the rim of the rocky outcrop that overlooks the pool, legs hanging over the precipice. His fingers are numb inside his gloves. His mother would bite her own hand off and swallow it whole, if she saw him up on the cliff.

There's a figure beneath him. No, two. The girl with platinum-blonde hair arrives with a guy Roland has never seen before. They release each other's hands and sit near the pool. Three others follow. He recognises some from the bus. One has a guitar slung over his back.

Roland waits until he sees Damien walk up Morley Lane. He takes in the swing of his hips and the luminescence of his shoulder-length hair. As the boy approaches the others, Roland anticipates the breadth of his back beneath the denim jacket. It's hard to see details from where he perches, especially in the murky winter light, but he takes in what's necessary. The pierced ear, studded leather belt, Motörhead embroidered on the back of his denim.

They like the same music.

Roland walks down the incline. His shoes hiss in the grass. Clusters of red-capped toadstools beckon under the leafless trees to his left. The moment couldn't be more perfect. Roland waits until Damien sees him, raises a palm and drops it by his side. He walks to the others, oh so casual. His heart gallops like a train.

The train is about to enter a tunnel. Dark and fast.

Bottomless

They've been at the water's edge long enough to sink some beers, and for the cold to start biting. Roland sits between Damien and the girl with platinum hair.

He knows most of them by sight from the bus, seven altogether, wrapped in jackets, coats and scarves.

The light is thin, the sky the colour of ash.

People say the pool in the abandoned quarry is deep, real deep.

A guy in a long coat rolls a joint. The wind picks at tufts of tobacco, and blows strands across the water. Long-coat lights up and draws a few times, then passes the joint to a boy with a cheetah printed on the back of his denim jacket.

Roland has never smoked dope. He hopes his mother won't smell anything.

"Draw on it, Stevie, or it'll go out," long-coat says.

Stevie echoes a cough, passes the sputtering joint to Damien. Stevie coughs again, takes his guitar and strums three chords, out of tune and repetitive.

The platinum girl has brought a radio. Stevie's music clashes with her pop songs, metallic thin sounds, barely recognisable as music.

Albie, the shortest guy, tosses an empty beer can at Stevie, says, "You can't play for shit."

The boys roll on the grass, shouting, fists clenched. But they laugh as they lash out at each other.

The cold seeps through Roland's jeans to his backside, but he doesn't mind. He doesn't mind at all.

When Damien passes him the joint, he cups it in his hands like he's seen the others do. He draws the smoke in, and waits for something to happen.

He passes the smouldering stump to the girl.

Roland wishes he could pick a fight with Damien, so they could roll in the grass together, but he doesn't know how. And anyway, he wouldn't want to get that close to him with all the others round. Later.

And he doesn't want to fight with Damien. He never wants to fight with him.

Albie pulls his jacket tight around himself, and stands up.

"S'gettin' dark anyway," he says. "I'm off."

Stevie stands and slings his guitar over his back. Long-coat tosses a handful of stones into the blackening water and joins him.

"We're off too," Stevie says. "Said we'd be at Maz's before dark."

The platinum-haired girl stands to hug them goodbye, then sits next to Damien and touches his elbow.

"Hey, d'you want to come see *Tommy* with me tomorrow?" she asks.

Damien looks past Roland at the boy she came with.

"Don't you want to go, Andy?"

Andy puffs his chest, pulls the zipper on his leather jacket down to expose his Led Zeppelin T-shirt. "Already been," he says.

Roland wonders whether Andy is cold.

"Yeah," platinum adds. "He went without me."

"My brother took me. For free," Andy says.

"And you didn't ask if I could come too." The girl pouts and leans toward Damien.

She's trying to make her man jealous. Roland thinks she probably doesn't really *like* Damien. But what if she does? Worse still, what if he likes her?

Andy stands and kicks dirt into the water. He plants himself near the girl.

"Didn't think you'd like it, Sharon," Andy says.

"I – "

"Nah," Damien butts in before the girl can reply. "I saw it when it first came out."

"What did you think?" Andy asks.

"Yeah, good."

"Hey!" Andy pokes Sharon and giggles. "I wonder if Stevie knows the chords to *I'm Free*."

"He might *know* them," Damien says, "but that doesn't mean he can *play* them. He's a complete spaz on guitar."

Sharon laughs.

Damien laughs with her.

Roland wishes he wouldn't.

Andy fixes an arm around Sharon's shoulders. Every time she smiles at Damien, her boyfriend pulls her closer, like he can feel her slipping. He tries to kiss her, but she shuffles away and leans against Damien.

Some say the pool is bottomless, but Roland knows there's no such thing. He could push Sharon in; weigh her down with rocks and see if she disappeared. Then he'd know.

Damien twists and shuffles, reaches into his pocket for cigarettes.

Sharon's radio sounds awful, crackly, like the batteries are running flat. She stretches towards it and turns it off.

"You take that fuckin' radio everywhere. It sounds like shit," Andy says, nudging the transistor with his toe.

It's cold. Roland folds his fingers inside his gloves. The water is black treacle now.

Damien lobs a stone in. Smooth ripples propagate outwards.

"Oy! Where you going?" Andy shouts when Sharon stands and fastens her coat.

"Away from you!" she says.

Their shouts echo off the steep granite walls.

Roland wonders why they are a couple.

Damien has a pile of stones at his feet. He's trying to skim them across the surface of the water, but they sink with a single *plop*.

Sharon crouches for her radio, but Andy grabs it first and hurls it into the middle of the pool.

Ripples spread out, lapping the water's edge. The girl's mouth opens and closes.

Roland feels the heat of Sharon's tears when she rushes past.

He looks at Damien, and Damien looks at him. They look at Andy, who holds both his hands up, as if to say, *what did I do?*

"Think you'd better go after her?" Damien asks. Andy furrows his brow into a frown but leaves anyway, small shuffling steps, breaking into a run.

Roland and Damien are the only ones left.

Damien shifts so their thighs touch. Roland hopes the grey-green dusk hides his blushes, but he doesn't move.

He lifts his face and catches a hint of a smile reflecting his own.

That's when he knows.

Raincoat

The last streaks of teal sky darken to charcoal.

"So," Damien asks Roland, "have you read *Dune?*" It's almost fully dark, and cold as iced Pepsi.

Roland knows he should go, but can't leave. Not yet.

"Nah." He stares at the guy's hands. His forearms. His knees. Anywhere, except somewhere he shouldn't. "Don't get much time to read for fun."

"What *do* you read when you can?"

"Picked up something called *Dhalgren*. You know the second-hand bookstall at the market?"

"Far out! I really dig that book."

"Cool!"

"Sure is." Damien's Zippo makes its *curlink* sound, as he lights a cigarette. He taps one out of the box for Roland. His fingertips are golden fire.

"Cheers."

"How far through are you?" Damien's face is momentarily illuminated by the lighter's halo.

"I'm at the part where he's just — you know — with the guy?" Roland catches the glint in the other boy's eyes before the flame dies.

"Oh man, the guy in the leathers?" Damien's sigh is a jagged shudder.

"Yeah." Roland's gaze shifts from the other boy's knees to his thighs, to the dark ground between them. He dare not look upwards. The wind whips an orchestra of sound in the trees. The pool is a tar-black plate before them.

Roland relives the scene in the book; two guys clawing at each other, the sounds, the smell, the taste — *Oh shit!* He moves his hands over his belly and then lowers them. He doesn't want Damien to see what's happening. Not yet. Not until he's sure.

"And the wide red sun," the boy says, "the dying sun that rises and sets in the same place? Fuck. What did you think that was about?"

"Man, I loved that. I dunno. An evolving world? Possibility?" Roland's discomfort eases. "And the clouds clearing to reveal the two moons. That blew my mind." He looks up and tries to discern the other boy's features in the non-light.

"And what about the poems?"

This guy really wants to know what Roland thinks. Like he cares.

The longer they talk, the more certain he is. They talk about films and albums. They talk about school. They talk about love.

Damien leans over, lights another cigarette for Roland. He smells of patchouli. He slips the Zippo into his jeans pocket, but keeps his head close.

"Do you," Damien asks, "do you — have you ever? You know, with another — " There's a rustling behind them, and then a voice.

"You guys still here?"

It's Sharon, the girl with platinum hair. Roland wonders why she always gets in the way.

"Hey Sharon," Damien's voice is creased with concern. "You all right?"

For a moment Roland hates the girl. He hates her, until he realises she's crying.

"Andy's a bastard." Her voice is torn and rusted. "He ran off and left me."

"Where?" Damien rises, places a hand on her shoulder.

"I hate him." Her vowels are elongated with grief. "I never want to see him again," she wails, "and I'm sure I saw someone." She tells them she saw a man dipping in and out of doorways, diving behind a holly bush as she got nearer. "I turned and went the other way," she says. "But I heard him. He was following me," she sobs. Damien puts his arm around her. "And when I turned around, oh my God, his eyes." She struggles to get the words out. Roland isn't sure which way to look. "He was wearing a raincoat," she cries. "I just ran back here."

"Oh fuck," Damien says. "Do you think — "

"That guy?" Roland says. "The raincoat man? I've heard he only goes for boys. You'll have been safe," he says. It's the first time he's actually said anything to Sharon.

42

He only goes for boys.

He understands why Damien elects to walk the girl home. He likes him all the more for his chivalry, but the disappointment of seeing him go sticks in his gullet like a tumour.

Shit. Roland spits the word out under his breath. It's almost dark. How long has he been here?

Roland doesn't run, but he walks fast. His footsteps echo on the pavement.

There's no one else around.

And then there is.

He looks back over his shoulder.

No one.

Roland quickens his pace.

Tap-tap, tap-tap, tap-tap, the uneven gait of someone with a limp.

He looks back again, but no one's there. The sound stops. Roland stops. Where is everyone? Some houses have lamps burning, the blue flicker of television and the iridescent glow of Christmas lights visible through windows.

Roland starts walking again. The footsteps start again.

Tap-tap, tap-tap, tap-tap.

Raincoat.

Roland isn't scared.

At first he's not sure what the feeling is.

He slows his pace.

He's not scared.

He's excited.

Roland slides his key into the door.

His mother's gondola basket is sitting on the table. It's empty.

He glances at his watch. He's been away three hours. His mother walks in, her face tight. Her lips turned downwards, eyebrows folded towards her nose.

And then the questions start.

Punishment

Roland's mother says he's not allowed out of the house for two weeks.

"But – "

"No buts. You disobeyed me."

"I'm nearly sixteen years old."

"I don't care if you're nearly sixty, you will not disrespect me."

"All I did was go for a walk."

The slap doesn't sting as much as he expects it to. Perhaps the fear of being disciplined is greater than the punishment itself.

He thinks it will be a relief when the school holidays are over.

Until then, it's just him and her.

There will be mock jollity when her friends arrive for fondue and mince pies on Saturday. Then Roland will have to endure Christmas with just the two of them. He wonders whether the wooden silences will cease when they pull crackers at lunch. Or will his mother cancel festivities altogether because of his indiscretions?

He wonders how much longer she can do this to him. Margaret Underwood is not a large woman. Not strong. He could easily –

But there's no point dwelling on things that will never happen.

In his bedroom, Roland flicks his book open to where the bookmark is. Then he turns back several pages and re-reads the part he has read six or seven times already.

He closes his eyes and sighs.

This is Roland's world.

Secret Bubbles

Roland fills the tub on Saturday night, adds too much of his mother's *Three Wishes* bubble bath. He steps into the swirling water and is enveloped in foam.

He explores his anatomy with the competency of an expert beneath the creamy surface. Waving froth laps the sides of the tub in concert with his turbulent rhythm.

Afterwards, Roland strokes his skin and imagines it belongs to someone else.

The air is crisp with anticipation. Condensation mists the black of the bathroom window. He's sure something will happen tonight.

Roland scrubs his body with his mother's loofah, inhales the scent of her lavender soap. He visualises what he'll do later, when he's been banished to his room after his mother's guests arrive. He can sense bracken crackling underfoot. He can make out Damien's shape in the gloom of the winter evening. The odour of atrophied vegetation is more real to him than the hot cinnamon aroma of his mother's stollen that penetrates the crack beneath the door.

The doorbell rings. The guests are arriving. Soon they'll spear skewered cubes of bread into melted cheese. Soon Roland will climb out of his window, cautious into the moonless night.

The bubbles die away to reveal the murk beneath. The water grows tepid around the firmness of his body. Roland steps out into a warm towel. He leaves the steam of the bathroom.

His mother has transformed their home with coloured lights. A bubble of laughter percolates up the stairs. Clinking glasses. Christmas carols.

Roland has a monstrous appetite. But it's not stollen he wants to pass his lips on this holiest of nights.

Ten O'Clock

It hadn't been hard to find Damien's number in the phone book. Roland rang on Thursday night when his mother was in the bathroom.

His surname was Carrington. He lived on Anson Road.

"Hello?"

Roland was relieved to hear the boy's voice. He was glad no one else in the house had answered. A mother? A father? Brother? Sister?

"It's Roland. You know, from earlier today. The quarry?"

Damien didn't say anything.

"Roland from the bus?"

"Oh hi!"

There was a crackle, but no click. He hoped his mother wouldn't return to her room and eavesdrop before he said what he needed to. He'd call once, maybe twice from her phone. Then they'd find other ways to communicate. He was sure Damien would want to find a way.

"Just thought I'd call, in case, you know, you wanted to hang around together."

"You found my number."

Oh Shit. Did he seem too eager?

"Wasn't hard. Not many Carringtons around here."

"Nah. Guess there aren't many Underwoods either."

Damien had remembered Roland's surname. He tried to keep it casual.

"D'you wanna do something Saturday night?"

"Sure. Where?"

"The pool. Morley Lane again. Ten."

"All right, I'll be there. I'll bring a blanket."

"Blanket?"

"Yeah. It'll be cold."

"Okay. Good. See you then."

"Yeah. See you. And Roley — "

46

No one ever called him Roley. But after that he never wanted to be called anything else.

"Yeah?"

"I'm glad you called. Really. I wanted to talk to you again."

"You did?"

"Yeah. You know. About books and stuff."

Books and stuff.

Roley remembered their earlier conversation about a book, page-by-page descriptions of a man with another man. It had been like undressing each other using only words.

"Yeah. Me too."

"It'll be ace."

Those words had held the promise of something good. Something that might make Roley whole again.

Roley tucks cushions and a sleeping bag under his bed covers. Christmas music and the clink of glasses suggest the party's in full swing downstairs.

His mother will be having the time of her life, showing off her Venetian glass figurines, pouring sherry. She'll flirt with Mark, unless the senior partner's squirrel-eyed wife is looking. Mark is a toad of a man. He wears a dogtooth check suit and smells of fish. Roley is glad he was only expected to shake hands with them then retire to his room.

Roley's mother probably won't come into his room, but he can't take chances. He turns his radio on, the volume low. He sometimes listens to Radio Luxembourg before he goes to sleep. He turns his light out, opens the window. He has one leg out in the chill of the night air, one on the sill when a shaft of light enters his room.

"What the hell are you doing?"

Her *Charlie* perfume makes him gag.

She pulls him.

Everything darkens from the force of her blows.

There's only five minutes to go until ten o'clock.

Margaret's Legacy

When Roley's mother eavesdrops from the upstairs telephone, he usually hears a 'click'.

There'd been nothing when he'd called on Thursday.

She'd been in the house, of course. She was cross. She'd been decisive in the way she'd punished him for going out after dark that evening.

You will do as I say.

Not enough to make him bleed, though she had bruised him.

She'd been less careful when she'd found him climbing out of his bedroom window on Saturday night.

He examines his arm under the torch-lit tent of bedding, pushes on the skin to feel the pain again.

Crimson and burgundy blemishes in midnight torchlight.

His eye throbs.

If a fifteen-year-old boy is starved of companionship, he won't grow properly. Etiolated, with scant fluid running in his veins, he may wither and die. He needs friends, like the plants he studies in Biology need nutrients. He needs love for photosynthesis. And unlike what he's been taught in *reproduction,* that love isn't always for the opposite sex.

He needs to call Damien.

He thinks about using his mother's telephone again, adding another tuppence to her bill.

If he chooses his time carefully, it'll be worth the risk. If he can hear Damien's voice, if he can say, *sorry I couldn't meet you tonight, can we try again?* Another beating won't be so bad.

If he can speak to the boy he loves.

If he can tell him —

Roley aches. The hollow shame hurts more than cuts and bruises.

Damien will have waited for him. He will have paced by the pool in the abandoned quarry. He will have rubbed his cold hands together squinting at his watch, unable to tell how late Roley was, because it is a moonless night. Roley visualises the boy lying cocooned in the blanket he's brought.

Was Damien disappointed? Did he howl with frustration? Or did he walk away, back to the Charnwood estate?

Had he turned up at all?

Roley thinks about packing.

He must remember to take his best jeans. He'll use his holiday case, the one that lives on his wardrobe. The jeans have patches on the knees. He remembers his mother's frown when he last wore them. He'll leave the pair of polyester slacks she bought for him at half the normal price.

She always says he looks nice in those.

He tries to recall a time his mother didn't choose his clothes, tell him what to like, a time she didn't want to live his life for him.

Maybe when his father was around? The memory is laced with the cedar-wood smell of his Dad's aftershave.

But that was a long time ago. His father's face is hazy under the slow moving current of his memories.

What he does remember is the crunch of her foot on his eye socket, and wonders if she has cracked the bone.

He wonders whether she ever loved him.

His mother had been in a good mood on Saturday afternoon. Humming Christmas carols, she'd prepared food for her guests. She wiped crumbs from the mustard-gold work surface.

Roley had speared cocktail sausages with sticks and arranged them around an orange for her. It was something he'd enjoyed doing as a kid. He'd make spiral patterns and take five times as long as she would have. It's not something that appealed at fifteen, but he'd done it anyway.

She'd popped out when she realised she'd forgotten to buy Babycham for the ladies. Remnants of her *Charlie* perfume had wafted behind her.

Roley had picked up the paisley scarf she'd dropped, wound it around his neck and pulled tight, because his mother strangled him just like that, stifled his spirit. He pulled tighter until the pressure on his windpipe and the *Charlie* smell made him gag.

Margaret Underwood married beneath her. That's what Grandpy Nick and Nannie Grace said. Roland senior was a wastrel who flitted from one sales job to another, Grandpy said.

Roland's father drank heavily and put money on the horses, Nannie said.

Margaret was one year into a promising career as a lawyer when Roland senior got her into trouble, Nannie said, as if he'd dobbed her in to the police for stealing a library book, as if he caused the trouble all by himself.

Every time Roland looked in the mirror, he saw his father's features. A wastrel. A troublemaker.

Roland senior didn't hang around long enough to see his son start school.

They didn't know where he was.

The senior partners in Margaret's firm overlooked her when it came to promotion, a single mother, a disgrace.

Her words rang in his ears.

I work every extra hour I can. I do it all for you.

She would leave Roland with a string of strangers when he was little.

He missed her.

When he was older, he didn't miss her anymore. But by then, she wouldn't let him out of her sight.

Margaret sees a chance to redeem herself through her son. She sends Roland to the Grammar School, despite the exorbitant fees. He will want for nothing. She will give him the best upbringing she can.

Her son will study law at university. He will become a high court judge. He will marry a fine young lady and produce the requisite number of children.

He will not live in the Charnwood Estate with the lower elements of society.

He'll mortgage his soul for a house with three bathrooms and double-glazing.

Only then will Margaret Underwood live her life again. She'll feel success through her son's fingers. She'll see prosperity through his eyes. She will profit from her son's annihilation.

She will be saved.

Until then, she monitors his phone calls, and throws him onto the floor and kicks him when she catches him climbing out of the window on a moonless night.

Yeti

Several hours after his mother goes to bed, Roley decides to leave.

Waiting.

Breathing.

Pushed to the limit, no longer pinioned by this woman's net, he is ready to go.

His eye throbs where she kicked him.

Her cherry red nails peeping through the open toes of her satin slingbacks, inches from his nose.

Escape.

He lingers outside her door, senses his mother drifting into oblivion in her bed, then creeps downstairs, case packed, dressed like a yeti, multiple layers of clothing on his back.

There are piles of party plates in the kitchen. It's not like her to leave them unwashed. Perhaps she'd lost her impetus after she'd kicked her son in the face and blackened his eye.

Poised to leave, he stops by the telephone and dials Damien's number in a moment of preposterous spontaneity. He's memorised it since he first rang the boy he's desperate to touch. He's played the figures through his mind again and again since he rang the house on Anson Road on Thursday.

It's a crazy time to call, must be after four in the morning. Nearer five.

Knowing the light on his mother's bedside phone might give him away, he's about to disconnect, when someone answers.

"Hello?" A woman's shaky voice.

Roley had hoped Damien would answer. He had hoped to apologise for not meeting him the night before. He'd hoped to explain. He'd had an accident. He wouldn't tell him about his mother's shoe slamming into his face.

A door. He'd walked into a door.

Mother took him to hospital, kind loving woman that she is. That's why he hadn't turned up by the pool at the abandoned quarry.

Who knows, maybe they could meet later?

"Hello?" The woman's voice is shrill, barking. "Is that you?"

"Is he — can I?" Roley stumbles on his words.

"Who's there?" The woman's voice splits, like she's shouted herself hoarse. Maybe she's been crying.

Roley says nothing.

"Who *is* this? Is he there? Is he with you?"

"I — I just — " Roley swallows the words back.

"Who are you?" Her voice rises in pitch and volume. Alarm bells at a railway crossing. The distant call of thunder.

"Sorry. Wrong number." He clicks the receiver down, lifts his case, and walks out of the house.

Maybe he could go to Anson Road now. Wait until morning, or throw stones at Damien's window to wake him, only he won't know which one his window is. But if he can find him, maybe he can tell him he —

Roley lugs his case down the hill. What if he can persuade Damien to come with him? He imagines sitting in the cab of a truckie's van, Damien's hand resting in the gap in the seat between them, teasing his thigh with the slightest touch, signalling the heat of things to come.

It takes nearly an hour for Roley to walk to Damien's house with the case.

Perhaps he should apologise to the mother. Perhaps he and Damien could hang out. Maybe he could stay there until —

There's a police car outside the house.

Roland walks away. Quick as he can.

It takes an hour to walk to the motorway from Anson Road. It's longer than he thought. He stops every so often to shift the case to the other side, carting it like a lazy dog he can't leave behind.

He waits at the junction, lifts his thumb to the paltry number of passing vans. No one stops.

Why was there a police car outside Damien's house?

He thinks about where he wants to go, what he will do. He's so cold, even through the layers of yeti skin.

After an hour, he turns back and lugs his case home.

Sick Individual

Roley moves his spoon through lumpy porridge. Round and round. Metal scrapes on porcelain. He does it not to cool the breakfast down, but to accelerate the motion of his stagnant life. It's the first Friday of the New Year. He wishes time would pass faster.

He's been caught in a loop of uncertainty since the last Sunday before Christmas. The acid in his stomach is dissolving his insides. Maybe he has an ulcer. Perhaps the acid has leached out and made a hole in his heart.

His mother twists the aerial on the transistor radio. He doesn't listen anymore unless she turns it on. The deejay plays *Bohemian Rhapsody*. It's been number one for eight weeks or more. Crazy.

"Ugh," his mother says, and changes the channel.

News.

He hates the local news.

Missing Sharpford boy Damien Carrington.

He's heard it too many times. Roley hopes for resolution before the end of the school holidays.

He has mock exams when he returns in a week. He's been secreting himself into his bedroom to cram facts about the English Civil War. It's been hard to study with everything that's happened. Confused feelings of danger, disaster, lust, anxiety and guilt crowd his mind. Most of all, guilt.

Did he lure Damien to danger?

What if he's dead?

Did Roley kill him?

Where are you? I love you.

Roley's tried to understand the complexities of simple harmonic motion.

He's read about gametes.

54

He practices speaking French into his cassette recorder.

Où es-tu? Je t'aime.

Every time his mother passes his room, she opens the door a crack.

Every time, Roley stands up and closes it in a choreography of rage.

At breakfast, there is a stillness to the light that falls on the mustard-gold Formica kitchen table. The lemon yellow walls glow, and orange floor tiles shout *look at me* underfoot. Roley contemplates the mix of wavelengths that combine to create such a cacophony of clashing colours.

The radio crackles because its batteries are dying.

The porridge clags in his throat. No amount of sugar can sweeten it.

His mother sits beside him and sips her espresso coffee, she seems to be proud of the experience. She bought the stovetop caffettierra in Italy, and it has elevated her.

"Stop making that noise with your spoon," she says, stilling Roley's hand, "it's rude."

"Really? Why?" The rage rises within him.

"I'm not going to argue with you," she says. "It just is. Anyway. I think they've caught him." She turns the radio up. The crackles and hisses are amplified, but the words are no clearer.

... A man is helping police with enquiries ... identified as Terrence Waters of Morley Lane, Sharpford ... Detective Alan Preston confirms bodies ... too early to speculate ... missing Sharpford boy Damien Carrington, or sightings ... referred to as 'raincoat man' ... a 'significant development' ...

"This is why I tell you not to go out, Roland," his mother says. "This is why I try to keep you safe." She tuts. "So close to home."

Roland stirs his porridge again, though the lumps in his bowl are grit compared with the pebble in his throat.

"He's a sick individual," his mother continues. "It's an illness that man has. An illness. Even so, he's not fit to live."

For once, Roland nods and agrees with his mother. He swallows another mouthful, along with the tears that brew inside him.

Raincoat Man

Following the arrest of a Caucasian male, aged 69, on the Friday 2nd January 1976, East Midlands Constabulary has issued this statement.

A man is helping police with enquiries relating to the disappearance of six Leicestershire schoolboys aged between nine and sixteen spanning a period of eighteen months from May 1974 to November last year.

The man has been identified as Terrence Waters of Morley Lane, Sharpford.

Detective Alan Preston confirms the bodies of five young males have been found at a property at Morley Lane.

The bodies have yet to be formally identified and next of kin notified.

Detective Preston says it is too early to speculate whether this development is related to the case of missing Sharpford boy Damien Carrington, or sightings of an elderly male variously referred to as *raincoat man* or the *black shadow*, responsible for attacks on young boys in the area since June.

Detective Preston, who led the investigation into the case of the missing boys, refers to the arrest as a *significant development*, as the search continues at the property on Morley Lane and surrounding area.

Ends.

Wastrel

"Take your elbows off the table!" Granpy Nick roars at Roland.

The table is so high the little boy can almost rest his chin on it, though that would likely earn him a slap.

He wishes adults would tell him off for the things that mattered. For things that hurt, like slapping, or spitting in people's faces.

Surely those are worse than elbows on the table?

They can't have told Mummy off enough about hurting people when she was little, because she hurts him all the time.

She Loves You comes on, and Nannie Grace turns the radiogram off.

"We don't want any of that rubbish playing while we're eating," she says. Nannie straightens Granpy's tie, pulls her chair from the table. Her bum settles onto the basket-weave seat. A napkin is placed on her lap. She tilts the spoon into the yellow of her soup and lifts it to her lips.

There is a right way and a wrong way to hold a soupspoon, Nannie points out to Roland.

He doesn't think that's the right thing to do with any sort of spoon.

"What's the matter, don't you like it? Look there's a spot on your chin — best wipe that off — "

"Leave him be," Grandpy says. "That child looks like a ragamuffin anyway. It's the way he's made."

"I cannot abide soup on a person's skin," Nannie says. The serviette is harsh linen. "When Margaret arrives we must tell her what the boy did."

Nannie says *the boy* when she doesn't want Roland to know she's talking about him, like it's some other five-year-old she's picked from the street.

"What's that?" Grandpa asks. "What did he do?" His words are separated by spoonsful of soup. He could put the flames of Nannie's words out with a barked command if he dared. But he doesn't. He adds paraffin to them instead.

"It's not right, what the boy did," she says, as if he's not in the room. "It's a perversion."

Roland's feet don't reach the floor when he sits on the tall, tall chairs. Every time Nannie says another thing about him, something in his tummy melts. He shrinks a little more.

"Yes, I'm sure it is," Grandpy adds.

Roland's grandmother's words are like a forest on fire. It's hard to put a stop to them. They leap up when you think they've gone.

There's always a lot of smoke.

When Roland visits his grandparents, there is space. There is time. Although he has a room to himself in his own house, that door is always open.

Here, he brings toys out of the little case his mother has packed for him.

The memory is fresh enough to sting.

He put black-haired Action Man's head over yellow-haired Action Man's lips. He made a smacking kiss noise with his mouth.

"I love you," he whispered. "I won't let them hurt you."

He changed his voice.

"Let's run away. We can live on my boat."

He changed his voice back again.

"Just the two of us. We can be married."

That was when his grandmother had pulled the toys from his hands, and hoisted Roland up by the ear.

She hurt him in ways that were hard to describe, hard to tell anyone about afterwards. She didn't use her hands for most of them.

"You're just like your father," she'd said. "You'll come to no good." The flames leapt and grew. "No, you're worse than he was." Nannie picked the toys up. "He may have been a wastrel," she'd snapped the black-haired head off its shoulders before tossing the carcass in the bin, "but at least he was a proper man."

The soup is yellow, but it tastes of pain.

Escape

Roley feels the house grow lighter without the weight of his sorrows. He leaves through the front door. She may not sleep through his departure, but his mother no longer has the power to stop him leaving.

He can't stop crying.

His steps mark time with metric precision. The footpath resonates with the tap of his sneakers. It shines with recent rain under the sodium glow of the third lamppost on the right.

The case is heavy in his hand. He packed six pairs of underpants and then put three back, partly to lessen the load. Mostly, because he doesn't know what's his and what isn't.

Everything he owns comes from his mother, a woman who sleeps lightly, though the weight of her punishments is hard to bear.

Even his body belongs to her, she says, because he came out of her.

He walks to Anson Road.

He doesn't know why he still goes there, what he's hoping to find.

It's hard to know what you're looking for when you're fifteen, and the world is full of wonder but dangerous and unforgiving.

He doesn't know what to do.

Right now, he can barely keep it together to stay alive.

He heads back home just as the sun is rising.

Maybe he'll try again tomorrow.

Bread

It all comes down to bread, Roley thinks. The key is stiff in the door. He wiggles it, careful not to make a sound.

He looks at himself in the hallway mirror, puts his hand to the fading bruise under his eye.

He tiptoes up the stairs, turns the bedroom doorknob with the precision of a person diffusing a bomb, and he's inside. He sheds the outer pair of trousers, both of his coats, the scarf and hat. It's warm in his room after the biting cold outside.

He's tired, but he can sleep all day. He's not at school and his mother's back to work.

The hum of the plumbing tells him she's showering.

If he'd had the nerve to follow through with his plan, he'd be hitchhiking south on the motorway now, his mother oblivious to his absence.

If he'd done it weeks ago, he might have run away with Damien.

But there is no Damien. There never will be.

He's blown the chance he had with the boy he loves. The boy he said he'd meet by the bottomless pool on a Saturday night, but failed to show up.

The boy who might be dead.

In the blue-white light of day, he unpacks the case, and questions the sanity of his actions.

Roley's fresh bruise throbs.

He can't stay here with her.

But he can't go. He has to eat.

Money is the route to all disaster, but man cannot live on air alone.

He needs bread.

He's too tired. He's too sad.

Maybe he'll try again tomorrow. Maybe he won't.

Two Foot Deep

They find Damien's body in a grave two-foot deep.

Roley hears it on the national news.

Terrence Waters (69) of Morley Lane, Sharpford is helping police with their enquiries.

He is Raincoat Man. He is evil incarnate. He is the *sick individual* Roland's mother uses to scare him.

Waters describes where he has laid Damien to rest. The soil is densely packed near the old quarry. Penetrating it is like breaking cement.

Roland calculates how long it takes to dig a hole that deep, that wide, that long. He imagines dirt filtering through the gold of Damien's hair, scouring his lips, soiling his sleeping eyelids, eyes that will sleep forever.

Did Terrence Waters take a shovel with him, or did he go home to fetch it after he'd suffocated the boy? Was Damien too heavy to move? Almost an adult. Were his other victims lured into the house on Morley Lane or carried afterwards? Was Waters too lazy to murder further away from home? Did he use power tools before he secreted parts in voids behind walls and underneath water heating cylinders? Did he kill the fish before he filled his ornamental ponds with concrete and flesh?

Roland's sadness is too hard to hold, too big to see, too deep to feel.

When school starts, his mother promises she won't let Roley out of her sight. She will ferry him from door to door. She will change her job. He'll never have to go on the school bus again.

Oh my God. You knew that boy?

A little. He travelled on the same bus.

Oh my God, it could have been you, Roland.

I guess.

*

He'll never travel on the bus again, where the Grammar School boys don't speak to the College School kids. They'll barely speak to each other. But there will be resignation in their silent looks, unspoken sympathy, their rivalry stilled by the audacity of recent events.

Glass

"Come with me," his mother says.

Roley should run, out of the door, out of her life.

He shifts sideways and ducks, tries to pass, but his mother is too fast. She grabs him by his anorak hood and slaps him. Again.

It's been happening too often. Sometimes he starts it. He knows he does. But everything is her fault. Everything.

Except he can't tell her. She can never know what she's done.

He wasn't somewhere he should have been because of her.

If he'd met the boy from the bus on time, maybe he could have saved him. Saved the boy he'd fallen in love with.

Now the boy is dead, and it's all because of her.

She asks him to wash the dishes. He screams. He lashes out at her when she tries to reach out to him.

There's just the two of them in a house.

Just the two of them.

Can't she tell he's breaking inside?

"Why can't you talk to me?" she says. "Tell me why you're so sullen?"

"Fuck off." He says it so softly, he's surprised she hears him.

"Why you — " She chases him out of the room, captures him in the hallway. She lashes out at him, and the mirror crashes from the wall. He grabs her wrist.

"Don't even try," she says, and twists his arm for good measure.

Shards of broken glass crunch underfoot.

He should run. But where can you run to when you're fifteen-years-old?

He's read stories about runaways. Drugs, prostitution, violence.

His ambitions don't run high, not as high as his mother's are for him, but they run higher than a life on the streets.

He wants to be safe.

He wants to be loved.

He wants to be somewhere else.

Roley thinks about the boy. He must have waited by the bottomless pool on Morley Lane, where Roley was supposed to meet him.

He had said he'd meet him at ten.

He would have run past his mother that night, dodged her blows, risen from her high-heeled kicks if he'd had enough courage, if he'd known what not going would cost.

But he didn't.

It's not his mother he hates.

It's himself.

When she goes out to post letters, he walks to the pool, as if by going there now he can turn time backwards.

The air is crisp, pine-scented. It covers the smell of his disappointment. He feels it in his skin, his bones, his knees.

Breaking a mirror brings bad luck. The fear in the vault of his stomach will surely last longer than seven years.

The Pond

The pond isn't there anymore.

It's dried up, the water gone.

It never was bottomless, but then he never really believed it had been.

He often visits the pond in his dreams. But now it's not there anymore.

Herman's Song

Herman is probably the oldest person Roley's met since he came to London. None of the kids know how old. Some say twenty-four, some forty, others a hundred.

Herman has the sort of face that makes it hard to fix him to a place and time. It's a kind face, though there is sadness behind the laughter. You can see it, even through the makeup he wears when he is singing.

"Hey kid," Herman had said in a throaty European accent the night they'd met. "You ever need somewhere safe to stay, call me."

Lots of people said that to kids on the street.

Most of them didn't mean it.

The runaways were usually somebody else's problem.

Whenever Roley and the others managed to slip into the pub in Soho where the old queens hung out, they'd often be bought drinks. Usually a Bloody Mary, or a Snowball, so they got some nutrition with it.

Roley had talked to Herman when the singer had his break that first night. The guy had slipped a card into Roley's hand and jumped up to sing *Wooden Heart*.

The bouncer threw him and the other kids out when Herman was halfway through *Tears of a Clown*.

Spring isn't much warmer than winter, and the streets near the bridge are unforgiving. Roley passes his sixteenth birthday in a haze of rotten meat and cardboard boxes. A boy with a bag and some glue provides cloud cover. Oblivion hits him like a freight train, and he wakes up in someone's bed.

At least it's warmer there.

You don't carry a lot when you live on the streets. His holiday case is long gone, swapped for a night of forgetfulness. A rucksack Roley stole when he had enough belongings to hold onto has replaced it.

Several weeks after his birthday, he's on another bender. Three weeks? Four? Who's counting? It's been a hell of a night. He's paid for something more transcendent than glue with something more cherished than a bag. He's bleeding now, from several places. The warmth of his blood seeps into his clothes and cools rapidly. It's cold in the darkest part of night, even in May.

A song drifts into his mind, and he's not sure if he's alive or dead.

German words, an accordion's 'hee-haw' notes.

Roley finds the card tucked into a side pocket of the rucksack. He'd thought it was a business card, but when he turns it in his hands, studies it under the apricot glow of a streetlamp, he finds it's a ticket from one of Herman's gigs. The number is scrawled in black ink. A spidery hand.

Roley has a single coin left from the ones he collected at the tube station. He'd love a hot drink. Nothing's open. He has no idea what time it is.

The coins clink into the metal of the only working coin box. He's stripped many near the bridge himself for a bellyful's-worth of two-pence pieces. He hopes so hard the call will connect. His clenched muscles scream in pain from the beating.

"Hello?" Herman's baritone croak is raspy with sleep.

"You said, you said if − "

"Who is this?" A sigh. "It's not even five yet. Is that you kid?"

"Yeah. It's Roley. I think I'm dying."

"Scheisse! Where are you?"

"Near the bridge."

"Which bridge?"

"The one over the river." Something oozes out of him like black water.

"You know how many bridges there are over a river in this city?"

That's when the beeps go and Roley thinks perhaps he should call an ambulance. But his hands won't do what his brain tells them.

He slumps down the glass walls of the booth and listens to the rush of blood sweeping through his head.

Opium

Roley wakes to find a man's hand on his cheek. The bed is warm and the sheets fresh and unrumpled. He can't quite put his finger on what the difference is. They aren't like the nylon fitted sheets he had at his mother's house.

The light in the room is subdued, flickers up and down, on and off. There's little sound, only a *whirr, whirr, whirr*. Roley catches the hot smell of dust illuminated by shafts from the projector.

"What? Where am − "

"Don't try to talk," Herman says. His accent is deep with blunt corners.

Roley's insides hurt. His outsides too.

Herman wears a silk dressing gown with dragons in flight against a black sky. Roley thinks the dragons are red, but it's hard to tell in this light.

Herman sits on an armchair that is next to the − what? The couch that Roley lies on, yes, it's like an old psychiatrist's couch. He thinks the eiderdown is royal purple, though it's hard to tell.

"Doctor said you need rest. You will be fine. But rest now." Herman places his hand on Roley's forehead for a moment, as if checking his temperature, and then turns to face the flickering light.

"What is that?"

"A film."

"Can you turn the sound up?" Roley rasps. "I want to hear it."

"No sound," Herman says. "Was made before sound."

"How do you know what's happening?"

"Watch carefully. There are clues. Don't speak. Rest."

"Tell me what it's about."

"A doctor is trying to capture the medical benefits of opium." He pauses a second, as if searching the screen for a clue. "He wants to do this, but without the danger of addiction."

"How old is this? They had opium then?"

"1919. Yes, they had opium."

"That's crazy." Roley sits up to get a better view.

"But really it is a film about addiction. About love, infidelity, and murder. There is always a murder in films like this."

"Guess they don't need sound to show a murder."

"No. Passions ran high when they were making this movie. Almost there was a real murder."

"Really?"

"And infidelity. Much infidelity."

"Really. How do you know?"

"Because I was there."

That's when Roley sees the doctor's long face on screen.

It's Herman.

Prat's Curry

Herman asks Roley if he likes curry.

"I guess," he answers, uncertainty dogging his responses.

Roley doesn't have the skills to accept unconditional kindness. His head hurts. He looks to his left, then his right, as if he's expecting danger. He hasn't moved farther than Herman's bathroom in days.

"I learned to make curry in Belur." Herman points towards the setting sun through the apartment window, as if that is where *Belur* lies. "From a man named Albert Timmins."

Roley nods. He has never heard of the place. Perhaps it's in India. Or Pakistan. But Albert Timmins doesn't sound like a Pakistani name.

"Maybe he was a man. Maybe a saint," Herman continues, as if speaking to himself. "Maybe something else."

Hunger builds in Roley's gullet, clawing its way from his belly.

"Many beautiful temples," Herman adds, his voice throaty and accented. From the couch, Roley detects the scent of cinnamon and cloves. It's faint at first, but intensifies when he imagines the weight of food on his tongue. He's only managed soft puddings and milk for days. His jaw clicks in a fragile glass-like manner when he chews, yet all he wants is to taste one of his old neighbour's curries.

Roley never knew her name. His mother called her *Prat,* though he's sure that wasn't their neighbour's real name, just as the woman's husband wasn't really called David.

The neighbours' children were sullen and had little to say to Roley and his mother when they went over for dinner, yes-no answers and no smiles. The grandmother, David's mother, was a passing shadow. She'd eat her meal and spirit herself away before everyone else sat at the table, either too grand, or not grand enough to dine with the others.

Roley felt uneasy until they were seated at the table. Then he lost himself in a cornucopia of flavours.

"Have you tried this, Margaret?" Prat asked, manoeuvring a laden tray under Roley's mother's nose. When Roley bit through the crisp batter of a shrimp fry, his mouth exploded with flavour.

"We had used lettuce in this," Prat said. She spoke English well, though there was something off with her command of the tenses. Roley couldn't put his finger on exactly what was wrong, but he knew it wasn't right. But there was nothing wrong with the food.

"Do you like the meat curry?" David asked, filling Margaret's glass with Chianti.

"Lovely," Roley replied between mouthfuls.

"Oh good," Prat said. "I had been nervous all day. Worried the food might be too spicy." She pronounced it *narvuss. I had been narvuss all day.*

"No, I love it," Roley said.

"Your sari is beautiful," Roland's mother said, running her fingers over the silk on the loose folds on Prat's shoulder. The fabric shimmered blue.

"Thank you," Prat replied. "Just an old thing. One day I must show you the good ones."

One of the children snuck away and clicked on the television remote. David barked an order and she returned to the table to play with her food, dragging a fork through mounds of uneaten rice.

"Look how well Roland eats curry," Prat said, pointing her fork at him for emphasis. "You had eaten nothing." She scowled at the curly-haired girl.

Roley liked going to the neighbours, where his smallest efforts were good enough. All he needed to do was push the fork into his mouth, load morsel after morsel of fragrant flavours onto his tongue, and he'd be praised for it.

He took a risk.

He'd seen grandmother at the table earlier. She rolled rice in gravy with her fingers and lifted the ball to her mouth.

Roley tried it.

"Look. A proper Indian boy," David said. His mouth lifted at the corners.

"He knows how to eat rice like a proper nawab." Prat's smile was all the encouragement Roley needed.

He cleared his plate using his fingers.

Then he licked it for good measure.

David and Prat were delighted.

Roley's mother said nothing.

His punishment would come later.

Herman brings in a bowl of steaming curry and rice. The aroma takes Roley somewhere he hasn't been for a long time. He'd like to think of it as a pleasant memory. But when he recalls the beating his mother gave him after dinner with the neighbours that night, he doesn't think so.

Roley lifts the fork to his split lips and begins to cry.

Another Silent Movie

The flicker of a cine-projector illuminates the room. Intermittently. Roley leans sideways into Herman's arms, feels the prickle of the man's beard against his soft-boy cheek.

The only sounds are the projector's *thirick thirick thirick thirick* whir, the *heech* and *haaar* of Roley's intermittent sobs.

Herman holds the boy close and rocks him.

Their meals lie untouched on the table.

Roley doesn't know why he can't stop crying.

Sometimes too much kindness is hard to bear.

Since Roley arrived Herman has barely touched him; a gentle squeeze of his shoulder, a palm on the forehead, a supporting shoulder as crutch when he visits the apartment's tiny bathroom.

Herman shifts a little, as if unwinding a knot in his back. The movement is subtle, and difficult to interpret.

It's started, Roley thinks.

There are some things his mother was right about. She used to say *if something seems too good to be true, it probably is.*

Roley edges his arm down to the man's thigh, shifts his hand upwards. He knows what to do from months of surviving on the streets.

"No." Herman's voice is firm. He lifts Roley's hand away. "This is not what I want," the man says.

Roley hesitates.

"It is not what you want either," he continues.

"What do you want?" Roley asks. "Why did you bring me here?"

"You were hurt," Herman says. "I helped." He returns to the arm-chair. "Now eat," he lifts the fork to his mouth. "It's good."

Roley makes fast work of the meal. Herman is right. It *is* good.

"Then we will watch another movie," the man says.

Another silent movie. Another day when Roley is safe.

He wonders how long it can last.

The Note

Three days after Roley slips away from Herman's apartment, he finds the note. It is written on pale blue *onionskin* airmail paper, the sort his mother uses to write to Aunt Jane in Canada. The note is neatly folded in an unsealed envelope, along with a fiver. It is tucked in the side pocket of the rucksack, the one he hardly ever uses. The ink is watery blue. He moves deeper underneath the bridge, so spots of summer rain don't destroy the words before he reads them.

CONTRACT
BETWEEN
HERMAN SCHILL
AND
ROLAND UNDERWOOD

This Contract, by and between
HERMAN SCHILL
hereinafter referred to as "Herman" and
ROLAND UNDERWOOD
hereinafter referred to as "Roley", is for the purpose of providing support and succour.

- If Roley is hungry, he should remember not all nourishment comes from food.
- If Roley is lonely, he should know not all friends are what they seem.
- If Roley is cold, there is warmth in the comfort of only some strangers.
- If Roley finds he wants a way back, some can show the way.

Your friend,
Herman.

(And, no, I am not a hundred years old, though not far off.)

Slips Through the Cracks

Though he has sex on a regular basis, like most of the people he knows, Roley is still waiting to make love for the first time.

Dead Weight

He often stole when he was living on the streets. It was their reality, their story. The scraps falling from society's table weren't enough to keep them alive.

Since Roley's been living at Appleby Towers, life isn't much easier.

He misses his friends. Some of those *friends* would rob him, and beat him for the coins he'd collect, but they were the only people he had.

He goes to the soup truck on Monday.

The volunteers have sussed out it's someone's birthday, and there's cake. The dude with the limp has fresh batteries in his radio. The music is tinny and scratchy. Someone's dancing. Roley misses this.

He thinks about the time some kids from the school bus listened to a radio beside a bottomless pool, so long ago. A girl with platinum hair had a fight with her boyfriend and the guy lobbed her radio into the water. Roley remembers talking to a boy with corn-coloured hair. After everyone else left, the boy had leaned in towards him, and he'd felt his life was about to change.

But it never did.

"D'you want this?" A guy thrusts a plate towards him.

Roley nods his thanks. His benefit ran out three days ago. There's another three days to go until the next payment comes. There's hunger in his belly and his heart.

The first time he robbed was with Dusty, a guy from under the bridge. Dusty had a dog called Bones to keep him warm and provide other services. The dog needed a big tin of Kennomeat a day. It shat large sausage-shaped turds that people were always walking through. Dusty always needed more cash to keep Bones alive.

"They left some stuff in *Pennymore* when it closed down. Shame to let it go to waste," Dusty had said one cold night.

"So, what're you thinking?" Roley asked him.

"Tonight, after it gets dark." Dusty mimed lifting with his hands. "Back entrance. I need someone to help carry the goods."

Where was the harm in it? A victimless crime.

They'd come out with two shopping trolleys full of stuff neither of them needed. They had to abandon both when a security guard had appeared and shouted, "Oy!"

But Roley hadn't come away with nothing. He'd watched what Dusty did with the screwdriver and how easy it was to slip the Yale with a piece of plastic. He'd come away with knowledge.

They'd done a few more places before Dusty and Bones disappeared.

"Moved on," an old guy in a greatcoat had said.

Roley had been in Appleby Towers a week when the need first arose. The benefit was never enough even without dope and other provisions he'd acquired a taste for on the streets.

In some ways it was easier by himself. He was less visible, like he could make himself into a gas and slip between cracks and diffuse away unseen.

The apartment block is opposite Appleby. Half the flats are boarded up. The stink of piss in the stairwells is stronger, the graffiti edgier, the reggae beat deafening loud. Roley watches the tower from his apartment window. He goes over when it gets dark, doesn't have to wait long these short winter days. He gets a feel for the place, and then comes back.

This time he wanders around, screwdriver in pocket. It's a chunky heavy one he took from Wilkinson's a month back.

The flat's been empty for weeks. No lights. That could be because the electricity's been cut off, because they couldn't pay the bill. But there's been no other activity either. No movement in the

77

curtains. No sign of the bald man whose comings and goings matched the pattern of lights going on and off in that apartment.

Another victimless crime.

Roley counts the floors, his breath coming faster and raspier with each storey he climbs. No one else is around. The strip light on the landing flickers. It takes a minute, and he's in. Dark as a donkey's arsehole, and smelling just as bad. Roley guesses the bald guy left food to rot when he did a runner.

He clicks his torch on.

That's when he sees them.

The glint of eyeballs, inches away from his face. Silent eyeballs.

The bald man lunges at him.

Roley is knocked to the ground.

He struggles to breathe.

He can't speak, the man's hands around his throat.

I'm suffocating.

He can't see, his torch has fallen aside and rolled away.

His eyes are bursting. The man has pinned Roley's body with his own, his arse on Roley's chest. His legs pinion Roley's arms.

Roley throws his legs up, tries to shift the man with the thrust of his weight.

His right arm is freed momentarily, long enough to slide the screwdriver from his pocket. The man doesn't seem to notice. Roley's eyes have become accustomed to the faint light from his torch lying on the other side of the room, and he brings the handle of the screwdriver down on the man's head.

Once. Twice. Three times.

The man's grip loosens. His eyeballs do something weird. Those ghostly silent eyeballs.

Roley strikes again. There is a dull crack of something breaking. The man falls on top of Roley. He must shift the dead weight of him away.

The dead, dead weight.

Red

Red is the colour of the darkness of his eyes.
Red is the beginning and the end.
Red is yesterday, and all his tomorrows.

In the dim torch-lit void, Roley examines the black stains on his hands.

He is imprisoned beneath a sleeping body. Entrapped by bones and flesh. He kicks his way out. He swallows bile that threatens to spill over.

Red above. Red below.
Red in the heart of his diminished dreams.

He knows the body isn't sleeping.

In the dim torch lit void, Roley examines the black stains and knows the smears are not as they seem.

They are red.

Later his pleas of self-defence fall on deaf ears.
How could it have been self-defence when you broke into the man's apartment?
He tried to strangle me. I was suffocating.
But you broke his skull in three places.
Apparently Roley's mild bruising is not considered to have been life threatening.

How far does a killer have to go, before he's considered a threat to others?

Less than Roley thought. A lot less.

Sewing Mailbags

It isn't what he expected, but Roley's never thought much about what life in a young offender institution might be like. It's not the usual career path for a boy from the Grammar School. It's not what Margaret Underwood had planned for her only son.

He was destined to become a lawyer like her.

A judge?

A criminal lawyer?

A criminal?

He was destined to become a lawyer until he killed a man.

I want to do something else, he'd said when Margaret had insisted law was the path he should follow. But running sacking through the jaws of an industrial sewing machine hadn't been what Roley had envisaged.

When he arrived, Roley thought sewing mailbags was an impossible cliché, something that never happened in real prisons. He was wrong.

The hard guys take the soft jobs. The kitchen. The vegetable garden. Caring for animals in the prison farm. The newcomers are left with the dregs.

The screws are in on it too. The way tobacco and other goods change hands indicates who's helping whom and who's providing certain favours in order to secure rewards.

Roley keeps a low profile.

Because he's sixteen, he escapes the drudgery of work for several hours a day to study for qualifications he would have completed a year ago, had he stayed at school.

But the hours in the sewing area pass slower than those in the schoolroom.

His mother comes to visit.

There is a catalogue of dos and don'ts, should haves and shouldn't haves.

She hasn't changed.

The tearful phone call from a police cell after his arrest hadn't gone well. She'd discovered her son was alive and then flipped. She'd shouted at him, told him how irresponsible he was and what a disappointment he'd been. He hadn't heard the rest, because he'd held the receiver at arm's length.

Now she catalogues the sacrifices she's made. She's not sure why she's even come to see him, she says, after everything she's done for him, all the opportunities he's missed. Her tirade plants a seed in Roley's mind.

The *if onlys* begin next, and Roley wishes himself back in the workroom. The click-clack brurrr of the sewing machine is better than the moan-groan whine of his mother's voice.

He realises he has the ability to do something he never could before.

Roley tells Margaret Underwood not to visit him again. He tells his mother to never come back.

The Gift

Roley fears adult prison will be harder than the young offender institution.

His mother asks to see him before the transfer.

He refuses.

She writes to him, sometimes weekly, sometimes more often.

He learns she's sold the house.

He learns she's married again.

The husband breeds parrots.

He sounds like a twat.

He learns that they live on the Charnwood Estate.

He never replies to her, though he accepts her gifts.

She's sent his favourite chocolate, a single bar with ribbon tied around it.

He intends to throw it out.

When he bites into its dark depths, he is marked by the scent of defeat.

A Play

Roley runs an English class in the prison. The inmates listen to him. There are all sorts here, including paedophiles and wizened old bikers who have shot through the knees of their enemies with modified firearms.

They're writing plays, stories and poems. Roley brings something he's written, to show them how to structure a script.

Act One, Scene Four.

Dramatis Personae:

Robert: Fifteen-year-old boy who wears 'unbranded straight-leg jeans', anorak, plimsolls and gloves. His attire would be considered 'square' for the era (1975). He has a 'regulation school haircut'.

Damon: Fifteen-year-old boy with shoulder-length hair and denim jacket with *Motörhead* embroidered on the back.

Scene: Twilight. R and D sit on a grassy bank on the edge of a dark pool. A wall of sheer rock circles two sides of the water.

D: So, have you read *Dune?*
R: Nah.

Robert stares at Damon's hands.

R: Don't get much time to read for fun.
D: What *do* you read when you can?
R: Picked up something called *Dhalgren*. You know the second hand bookstall at the market?

One of the bikers reads the part of Damon while Roley portrays Robert. The biker is a slow reader. He reads:

One.
Word.
At.
A.
Time.

A Poem

Where are you?
I'm here.
Where?
Between the frames of a silent movie.

I look for you every day.
Keep looking.
I look every minute, every second, every hour, every year.

I waited for you.
I know.
You never came.

I tried.
But you weren't there.
I'm sorry.

You're older now.
You're the same.
That's what happens when you die.

I've been trying to find you.
Keep looking.
I am.
Maybe you'll find me in the end.

A Story

Being in and out of prison most of his adult life, Roley knows the system. The screws are in on it, too. Tobacco and other goods change hands. Roley knows who's helping whom and who's providing favours to secure rewards. It's a harsh environment. He sinks in the maelstrom of testosterone-fuelled savagery, and then comes up breathing for air, covered in bruises.

The trade in drugs, tobacco and phones is commonplace, but it isn't the only deviation from the rules.

Roley looks forward to Thursday afternoons. It's the only time he can get away from the nightmarish scenes in his mind.

The crack of bone.

The black of blood on his hands.

A dim light that shows little, but will haunt him forever.

This time, in mathematics class, Roley is re-learning calculus for something to do. It keeps his mind supple. The guy in the next seat struggles with the concept of powers and square roots. The man is silent with oriental eyes. Oh, he's quiet now, but when this guy cries *Mama* at night, his voice echoes through the corridor.

They share the class with blokes learning the basics of addition and subtraction. Increasing is the same as decreasing, until they are given the tools to identify the difference, though these individuals are not as dumb as they seem. They understand how to increase their status. They understand the rule of diminishing returns, and who to blame when it happens.

Sometimes those responsible get cut out of the deal. Sometimes they just get cut. There's a lot you can do with a stolen safety razor.

Roley steers his attention back to integration and is wary when *Mama* boy asks for help. There's one sort of integration Roley's not keen on. He will not become part of this group of misfits and common thugs.

Every time he's inside, he may be considered a criminal, but he knows he's not like the rest of them.

Sometimes Roley wishes he'd seen his mother before she died.

Most of the time he doesn't.

He stopped seeing all his family.

Grandpy Nick and Nannie Grace had said Roley would always be their grandson, but they couldn't reconcile what he had become with the man they'd wanted him to be. Nannie sent her final letter when he was in prison for a crime he didn't commit. She said she wouldn't visit anymore. She thought he would understand.

The men are allowed one recreational class a week, something that doesn't necessarily lead to a qualification or make them more employable.

They choose motorbike appreciation, learning the names of models they will never own through honest means. Some learn to use computers. Others learn to play guitar. Strangled, stilted chords penetrate the impenetrable wall and those guys become Jimi Hendrix for an hour.

Then there are those who choose nimbler tasks to perform with their fingers. But these men have a defined place in the societal web of the unit. They are the moulted skins of creatures they once were.

Roley looks forward to Thursday afternoons. The days when Roley taught classes in prison are long gone. He knows he's not like the rest of the inmates, but to everyone else, he is indistinguishable. Subdued by the system. The system he knows so well.

The tutor weaves magic into the pupils' work. He takes them to a different place. Roley learns to write without agenda. He imagines clear sky, the breath of the ocean.

"Why don't you write a story or a play?" the man asks. He is younger than the other tutors. His hair is Velcro short. He carries a phone in his jacket pocket, unfazed by the possibility of it being stolen.

"All right," Roley says. "I will."

Something passes between them. Their tacit complicity fills the room with sounds no one else hears.

Roley is allowed pencils and writing paper, and he fills lonely hours after his evening meal.

It's a story he's held on to for decades.

He's been trying to write it since his first offence.

There's someone called Robert.

Robert meets a guy called Damon on a bus. Damon has shoulder-length hair. He wears a denim jacket with *Motörhead* embroidered on the back.

In the fourth scene they meet on the bank of a bottomless lake.

Scene: Twilight. R and D sit on a grassy bank on the edge of a dark lake.

Two sides of the pool are circled by a wall of sheer rock. There is a sloping pathway leading to the top of the cliff, covered in bracken.

D: So, have you read *Dune?*
R: Nah.

Robert stares at Damon's hands.

R: Don't get much time to read for fun.
D: What *do* you read when you can?

Each Thursday he hands the tutor the next part of the story.

Each Thursday the tutor returns the previous instalment. There are scribbled notes in the margin about characterisation, about the structure of the dialogue. The tutor doesn't write too much, but shows his appreciation with his eyes.

"I want more. More writing like this. I want to see where this story is going." His hand lingers on the manuscript for a second longer than it should.

Roley thinks about a boy he met on the bus. He makes the story become what it should have been. And when he writes about the delicacy of Damon's touch, the softness of his skin, the pulse of their loving, he thinks of the young tutor's hands.

There is Light

Although there is no one to collect him, Roley is in a vibrant mood.

Things happened this time that never should have, and he's never wanted so desperately to be free.
Scores were unsettled.
Time wounded any pretence of healing.
He'd been caught between two devils, far from the deep blue sea.

Though he's been in and out of prison over the years, more in than out, he swears this is the last time. He's fifty-seven years young. This is a new beginning.

This time there is light.

This time, he'll get it right.

Damien walks beside him. He should be an old man now, but he's still young, still beautiful. His hair's still the colour of wheat.

"I'm learning the lyrics to *The Killing of Georgie*," Damien says.
"Really? Do you sing?"
"Only in the bath." The boy laughs.

Damien stretches his young fingers to touch Roley's older ones, but they disappear before the two can meet.

That's what happens to ghosts.

Dried Up

Roley throws his bag onto the verge and drops out of the truck's cabin after it.

"Scheisse!" The expletive is hissed under his breath. The truckie doesn't hear him. Roley's bad knee is giving him gip again. It's twisted and bends in a peculiar way.

The vehicle whirrs and joins the stream of traffic on the motorway. The cargo of logs jiggles, and then it's gone, swallowed up in a haze of bridges and belching vehicles that fart out air someone's going to breathe tomorrow.

The dog is silent inside Roley's coat. He rubs its head and wonders if it's hungry. His own stomach growls.

It's been what, nearly forty years since he was last here?

He passes an *Amey Roadstone* sign. The working quarries shit out gravel and dust floats into the air that already holds more particles than it ought to. The roar is deafening, but the dog doesn't stir. A fly buzzes uncomfortably close to Roley's ear. He swats at it with his fist, and then scratches at the scaly skin under his beard.

It takes nearly an hour to walk there from the motorway. Would have been faster but for his knee.

When he gets there, he finds everything's the same, but very different.

There's his old house, with new roof-tiles. The magnolia tree, once only as tall as his leg, now towers above the house. It's in full bloom. The flowers' sickly scent reminds him of his mother, so Roley turns away and tramps to Morley Lane.

There's a stone in his shoe.

The puppy stirs.

Yep. Same, same, but different.

He turns the corner and the pool is still there, only it isn't a pool any more. There's a layer of scummy mud at the bottom of a deep hollow. Not that deep really. They used to think the pool was bottomless when they came here all those years ago.

Roley sniffs the air for residues of the past. He thinks he catches the scent of Damien, but it's just a bit of nothing in the breeze.

He sits in the bracken, takes the sandwich from his bag, offers a piece to the dog, who has the grace to eat it in one gulp without begging for more.

Then Roley lies back in the afternoon sun, tucks his bag under his neck, takes his cock out of his pants and makes the dog lick it like he's taught him.

He creases his face in concentration, clenches his fists, and waits for oblivion.

The End

The water is black, so deep, if you fall in, you might never reach the bottom.

When he arrives, the boy's voice is a whisper, tempered by the rustling of leaves.

"I'm here," he says with his eyes.

"You came!"

"You always knew I would in the end."

A Benign Deity

This is the End

I will be reborn as a fish. Perhaps a cod, or something with an asymmetric eye. They have moved stones to bring me here.

But first I, Albert Timmins, must die.

I call out my father's name for the third time, my voice cockerel clear, my words extinguished before I can give them meaning, because this is what happens at the end: the passion, the hunger, the plays. This is the true meaning of betrayal. I didn't wait around long enough to pay the bill after the final supper. I would have left a tip, but who's counting?

Spreadeagled like a starfish, each appendage secured with metal ties, I contemplate how it has come to this.

To be abandoned when hope has died.

To Thomas, who picks at other people's meals.

To Petaluma, who was the fastest driver on the continent.

To Ra, who rose beneath the stars.

To Norman, Desmond and Patsy.

To Pillar, who robbed her own mother.

To Hager, who cried at sad movies, and beat his wife with a pole.

To Tim the sailor and Alissandre, who kept the bones of his lovers to build a raft.

Where are they now? Have they forsaken me? I am left suspended in my own disbelief. I had grown to love them. Now they turn away, marching to the rhythm of their own time. The past, the future tangled together, presented in homogenised unity. To stay that way for all eternity.

To Deborah, who eats crab with a knitting needle.

To February, who only washes her hair on a Monday.

To Roma, Semi and Sonja.

Shall I go on? I could tell you about them all, but there are too many. There were so many. And where are they now? To think, I have been loved so.

To Salma, Dmitri, and Xavier.

To Michelle, who will never know the truth.

To Rina, who has an element in the centre of her heart.

Can I recall all that has been said? And what hasn't been told? What lies hidden between the lines? Not now. Not now. My limbs. My eyes. My bones. The essence of my being is thrown apart. My carcass is to be fed to my creditors.

To Hector, frightened of spiders. In the end, we are all frightened of something. To know what we fear is half the battle.

To Jazzy, little Mary, Minnie and Holly.

Ah, I have always loved women too much. How many of them will remember me? To think of what I lose is too much to bear.

To Traminer, Goral, Stefani and Daphne, the sympathetic, unsympathetic landlady.

As the life trickles from my wounds, I think of the disciples I have met on my travels.

My virgin father. The scars from my surgery. None of it makes sense, but we live in times when there is little call for rationality.

The gifts they brought were single use plastic.

They predicted my coming, but I have always been late for appointments.

Trespass

"What the fuck are you doing, Albert?"

Daphne has a tongue on her that could scratch concrete. Her hair is bunched on her head into concertinaed soapsuds. Her knees poke out of the grey bathwater, her old, old breasts poke into it.

"You said I could call in on you whenever I liked," I say.

"Yes, but I didn't mean the bathroom."

"Well no, but — "

"Get out of here now, or I'll call the police."

"But — "

"There is no *but*. And look what you've done to the doorframe."

"I can mend that. Just need some matchsticks and a little epoxy resin. And you can't call the police. There's no telephone in here."

"Screw the telephone. I'll holler so loud, they'll hear me in China. And you wouldn't need to fix the door if you hadn't kicked it through in the first place."

Daphne's not really mad. I can tell. She carries on bathing, pouring a mugful of the scaly grey water onto her grey scaly head, so she looks like a seal for a moment, a grey seal, in a grey world. Then she manoeuvres her body from the tub, straight into a towel, so as not to reveal an ounce more flesh than she revealed in the grey bathwater. I glimpse all of this in the glass on the steam-filmed cabinet while I'm examining my face. There's a pimple the size of Vesuvius on my neck, just below the ear, not far from the operation scar. How big does it have to be before it's classed as a tumour? I won't show it to Daphne. Don't want any more surgery. No, thank you, sir.

My landlady's dressing gown, once white, is also the colour of the rapidly disappearing bathwater. She must have washed it with her darks. I turn to face Daphne, and she ties the cord into a double knot, closing the doorway to her wobbly body. Does she think I've never seen flesh before? I'm made of flesh myself. Or at least I was the last

97

time I looked. The spirit made flesh through the love of the father, or some other distant ancestor. I can't remember.

Daphne opens the window a chink to let the steam out. I always forget to do that, and she has a go at me for that too. I follow her out of the bathroom. We reach her bedroom, where she gives me a stern look.

"You can't come in, Albert. Go back to your room."

So I do.

I pass Norman a tray of glasses. It's as quiet as death in the *Pig and Whistle*. Norman sluices the empty steins in the washer. The rotating brushes gurgle like a tickled baby. I tell him about my unsympathetic landlady. He stops, holds a glass up.

"Albert," he says. "You've got to stop doing things like that."

"Like what?"

"You can't go into the bathroom when someone's in there."

"But she said – "

"Never mind what she said. Daphne is a good woman. She took you in after what happened."

"Happened with what?"

"You know what I'm talking about, Albert. It's not everyone that'll take someone on after a thing like that."

"Like what?" My head hurts.

"After what you did to your wife, Albert."

"My wife." Perhaps if I ignore the pain, everything will make sense.

"Daphne could put you out on the street as quick as you can say sixpence if you carry on."

"Okay. No more bathrooms." I say. "And what was that about my wife? I don't have a wife."

Norman sighs. He loves *his* wife too much. A woman like that could eat a man for breakfast and still say fifty-two hail Marys before lunchtime. He's making a mistake about me though. I don't have a wife.

"No, Albert. You haven't got a wife," Norman says. "Not any more."

I don't know what he's talking about.

98

"There're more glasses over there." He points with his nose.

I wander over to collect a pint glass from the windowsill. It's nearly time to go home. I'll see if Daphne wants a game of dominoes. I can knock first. Don't want to break the lock on her bedroom door, too.

Two in one day would be bad.

I'd need a lot of epoxy resin to fix that.

Anointed

An old guy walking down Victoria Road reminds me of Stefani Rodrigues. He's old, though not as old as I am. Some people say I'm sixty-eight, others think I'm decades older, but they're not even close.

Stefani Rodrigues had a brown-paper-bag face and matchstick legs. A strong wind could have blown him over. I remember his shoehorn ears and accented voice.

Rodrigues was an important man in my life. He had a role in making me what I am today. I remember everything he did in detail. Everything, up until the point he tried to kill me.

The Rodrigues had a butchers' shop near the university. They sold unidentifiable meats to students of various religious persuasions. Of course you couldn't do that now. Feed lamb to non-lamb eaters and you'd risk being filleted and quartered on your own butcher's block. The world is becoming more dangerous.

My initiation took place in the school chapel, Stefani my only witness.

"What are you doing here, Timmins?" he'd asked when he found me there all those years ago. The elastic twang of his words was enough to intimidate most of the younger boys. But not Albert Timmins. I was made of sterner stuff.

"God has called me," I told Rodrigues. "I'm staying."

"Pull the other one, you phoney," he'd said, raising his fists.

That was when I'd made the light shine. The raw yellow glow cast radiant fingers over the pews. I clicked the switch in my pocket, twisted some wires, gasped and fell to my knees. Rodrigues saw it, his mouth an open 'O'.

"Crikey," he said, dropping his arms to his side. "What did you do?"

"I am the chosen one," I said, and made the censer roll off the altar. "Another sign," I announced, trying to mask my own astonishment. I didn't know how I'd done it, and whether I could do it again, but I acted like telekinesis was my favourite pastime. I gave Rodrigues a look, to imply I could do the same to his head.

Within the year, I'd built a following. I raided Mum's old *Readers' Digest* magazines for stories about redemption and salvation, and regurgitated them with flair.

By September, there were rumours I could turn water into lemonade, levitate in the air, and locate lost rulers using the power of the mind. No one saw me *do* any of those things, but Stefani, my greatest devotee by then, catalogued each miracle that came to his attention in his hymnbook. By December, we'd reached fifty-three. Beneath *There is a Green Hill Far Away,* Stefani's scratchy words:

He turned an Opal Fruit into a frog.

I had a forty-five strong following by then. The teachers were poking their noses into my affairs. Comments were passed about taking the Lord's name in vain.

They never discovered any of our initiation ceremonies though. Stefani and I, wearing cloaks made from curtains we'd stolen from the drama department, would anoint each boy with mud taken from the riverbank. Stefani would chant, while I drew the sign of the holy tadpole on the novice's forehead.

In our twenties, Rodrigues and I were still at it. We recruited at bus shelters and the supermarket that stood in a row of shops whose names all began with 'W.' *Wilkinson's, Woolworths* and *Wallpaper Direct.*

I earned a pittance at my job in the hosieries. Stefani had a few more bob than I did. The Rodrigues family had expanded: a second butcher's (*World Meats*) and the greengrocers next door (*Witloof and co.*). They were making a mint. It was money we needed. So when Rodrigues senior bought the ironmongers too (*Wrought Eye-on*), my friend did some creative accounting. We took a twenty-five year lease on a stuccoed house.

Anyway, when this guy that looks like Stefani turns off Victoria Road and disappears towards the Richmonds, it reminds me of when *I* gave Rodrigues the slip, rather than the other way round.

Soon after Papa Rodrigues carked, the punters started shopping in the supermarket. The family fell on hard times.

"I need my investment back," Stefani said one night.

"Plenty of tithes coming in," I said, "but I can't pay you yet."

"I've given you everything I own."

"And I said I'll be able to return it. Double."

"When?"

"Soon."

"I need it now," he said, curling his fists. "End the lease."

What Stefani didn't know was that I'd already cashed in. I had plans, and the proceeds were already accounted for.

I'd already bubble-wrapped the icons, boxed the incense, and wrapped the candles and crosses. I'd sent the Holy Books forward. I had a one-way ticket to somewhere Stefani would never find me.

The train was due to leave at seven minutes past six a.m.

A taxi dropped me and my suitcase with twenty minutes to spare. The station was empty.

A weight landed on my shoulder, and then Stefani and I were rolling around on the cold cement platform. He gouged at my eyes. I kicked his groin. He called me a thief. I called him a miser.

The roar of the train caused me to turn my head, its bright light flaring like a small sun. That was when Stefani Rodrigues rolled me onto the tracks, right in front of the oncoming engine, which was speeding through to Nottingham.

It was in the papers the next day. I have a copy, though I have kept little else from that time. The police took my single suitcase that morning.

Man disappears into thin air in front of speeding train.

I don't know how I did it, and whether I could do it again, but I acted like it was something I did every day. I floated away into the gaps between the gaps, to start a new life, where no one knew who I was, but where to this day, they know I am the chosen one.

Thakur Baba's Omen

A young man with skin the colour of bagels approaches me after the session and begs an audience.

"Thakur Baba!"

"Yes, my son?" I adjust my robes. Tonight's final posture almost exposed my Marks and Spencer Y-fronts. I need to be careful.

"May I request a private session?"

"Why, of course, Goral." I wipe my brow with a towel. "Book through my website."

"I — I wondered if I could see you soon. Maybe tonight. And perhaps every week. After yoga." He struggles with the 'w' of 'wondered' and 'week'. I've never figured where his accent places Goral. Perhaps it's Eastern European; maybe somewhere further away, somewhere more exotic. All around us, my followers wrap their sweaty bodies in layers of fleece and Lycra, before they leave the cocoon of the studio.

"I don't mind what it costs," he says. "I can pay."

Now he has my attention.

So that's how my weekly sessions begin with this troubled boy.

I take the spindly youth through postures I've pilfered from a stolen library book called 'Yoga for Health'. Sometimes I invent my own asanas for a laugh. We talk afterwards, share wisdom over tea and biscuits. He looks at me with wide brown eyes and takes in the philosophical mumbo jumbo I've memorised from the Hare Krishna paperbacks I scavenged when I lived in a squat on Richmond Road with a North American Indian called Petaluma. Goral is keen and receptive. And he pays in cash.

I make notes on my iPad after he leaves the studio, so I can remember what I've said. I don't want to contradict myself.

Goral is a lost and questioning young man, a very wealthy one at that. Still, the hiked fees will go part way toward covering the extra heating costs. It's not cheap keeping the studio at forty degrees for an extra hour, Michelle reminds me, when I climb up to our flat after the second session. I make my final *namaskar* to the boy from the upstairs window, as he climbs into his father's car.

"I 'ope you're chargin' him double, Albert," Michelle says, pinning a napkin over my robes.

"More than double," I reply. The soup Michelle serves is delicious. "Have we any beer?"

After the fourth session, I make a fuss about the way Goral's English breakfast teabag has come to rest on the hand-shaped holder by the sink in the side room. It's cooler in here than in the main studio, but still as warm as a cow's vulva.

"It is an omen." I clasp Goral's hand in mine. I warn him about gold-digging over-eager girlfriends as we drink.

"I don't think that will be a problem for me," he says.

"Why?"

"Women," he says, that peculiar way he pronounces 'W' that makes me *vwant* to hit him. "Women are not my cup of tea." He points to his cup. He's picked the best china one, of course. How could I not have known he was gay? I must observe my clients more carefully in future. And modify my predictions accordingly.

"The teabag spoke in Hindustani," I explain. "It used a gender-neutral term. I mistranslated." Improvisation has never been my strong point, but I am rather proud of how I have rescued the situation.

"You are so wise, Thakur Baba."

Vwize. Ouch!

At the end of the month, I persuade Goral he must keep coming to me. He agrees. I buy Michelle a yellow jacket she's been eyeing up for weeks, even though it doesn't suit her, and book a Thai massage for myself.

On the sixth week, Goral is niggled and can't concentrate on the private postures I make up for him on the spot. I enjoy looking at the way his neck twists under my command.

Afterwards he tells me he has ditched his boyfriend.

"He was becoming an expensive habit," he says. "The West End shows, the bands, the fine dining." *Vwest.* Shivers.

I reinforce his decision, as I must, and gently steer him in the direction of further self-enlightenment.

Michelle and I will take a trip to Calais in the New Year. Best top up on the beers and cheap wine while we can. Bloody Brexit.

Goral is embedding himself into my brain. My inner voice hears my own words as *vwine vwhile vwe can.* I suppress a shudder, and do an internal calculation to assess how many bottles of wine each session with Goral equates to, while Michelle flicks the tellie over to watch a Western.

Vwestern.

Arghh.

Confucius

I've always envied Kent Traminer. He has everything I want. He is all that a young man around these parts ought to be: handsome, strong as an ox and not without a penny or two. When I see his horse and dray outside the Bellingers' place, I wander over to see what business he has there.

"Albert Timmins!" Papa Bellinger hollers as I secure Shi Yin outside their homestead. "What brings you here on this fine day?" My horse marks the dirt with her hooves, back and forth, back and forth.

"I've come to call on Beth. See if she'd care to accompany me to Hector Price's dance on Saturday." Fearing Traminer has the same plan in mind makes me bolder.

"Well now," Papa Bellinger says, rubbing his beard with tobacco-stained fingers. "Well now," he says again. "Looks like you may have to wait in line."

The hungry looks Kent had been giving Beth the day before would have made a whore blush. He was like a dog waiting to sink his teeth into a pound of brisket, his uncouth behaviour most unbecoming on the Sabbath, while the fine ladies of the parish stood around us. That blaggard Traminer has stepped ahead of me. Again.

Beth Bellinger had looked mighty fine in church. A posse of girls had milled around her after the service, admiring her wide-brimmed hat, fingering the satin ribbon on her bodice. Later, she approached cousin Ben and me at the stables. She'd admired the gloss on Shi Yin's coat.

"Like silk velvet. How do you keep her so well-groomed when you toil in the fields all day?"

"K'ung Fu-tzu teaches us the cultivation of virtue is to be valued above all else," I'd said.

Beth's mouth had opened, as if she were about to speak, though no words had passed her lips. Ben looked at me, his features a puzzle.

"Also known as Confucius, the great one teaches there are five relations a man has to pay homage to."

Cousin Ben had furrowed his brow, but Beth had looked upon me like I was some sort of God.

"Man and his father," I continued, listing the five pairings the Chinese showman had recited at the carnival a week earlier. I couldn't remember them all, but my imagination served me well, and I substituted my own for those I couldn't recall. "Man and his horse," I finished.

I'd smiled at her and led Shi Yin out of the stables, leaving Beth with a look of astonishment on her face. I knew I had entranced her, but it didn't pay to appear too eager, so I left her talking to Ben. I left her wanting more.

I rub my horse's glossy neck. It is the colour of burnt chestnuts.

"Tell Beth I called." I nod to Papa Bellinger, turn away and ride towards the inn. The sun is setting in the west.

It isn't long before Beth pushes through the oak door of the inn.

"I've come to fetch ale for Old Dmitri," she says. "He's sick." She shows me the flagon, but I know she came here for one reason. She will have shunned Kent Traminer. I know she wants to listen to my pretty stories. I plan to tell her how the universe was created from chaos.

Cousin Ben enters the inn not long after Beth. The swagger in his walk suggests he may have dropped into Molly's emporium on the way. Molly serves fine liquor, and has an even finer selection of girls on offer.

True to her word, Beth secures a cask of ale under her arm and leaves the inn. How could I have misread her intensions so?

Ben slops ale on the table and sits next to me. The frothing liquid sinks into the knotted grain.

"A fine looking woman, Beth Bellinger is," Ben says. "And the best cook in town."

Not Ben as well.

"I mean to make that woman my wife one day," he carries on, emboldened by liquor. "Mark my words, I shall."

I finish my drink and head over to Molly's. There is a particular sort of comfort a man can use on a day like this. I ask for the new girl, the dark-skinned one called February.

Molly tells me that girl is not available. February always washes her hair on Mondays.

I leave, my liquor unfinished, leading Shi Yin away into the darkness of this deep Monday night.

The Ballad of Albert Timmins

Holly Painter, late for school, walks in the shadow of her imaginary brothers and sisters. She dances in the morning. She dances in the bath. She dances as trains roar along the railway that runs near her home, her waist shimmying left and right.

Holly takes the bus that day, unaware she will never return to the holy bosom of mother, father, her family.

Holly takes her time in class, to erase the errors of her past. She writes slowly and deliberately about some guy she's heard about. In her head, a song pounds, the song that's been beating in her brain since she was small. Holly licks her pencil. They are asked to write the old fashioned way. Her cursive script is slow and rounded. Slow. She thinks much faster than she can write, and longs for the ease of a keyboard. The song plays in a minor key.

"The Ballad of Albert Timmins"

She writes the title.

"They called him Albert Timmins"

She writes it again.

"They called him Albert Timmins"

She has the end. Now she needs to complete the rest. As if he were an elephant, no one knows where Timmins went to die. Perhaps Holly can imagine a noble death for her hero.

"They sang a song about a man," she writes.

In her head, Holly is dancing the swift flowing movements of a girl who craves the love of strangers more than she should.

Here comes the rest.

The Ballad of Albert Timmins

They sang a song about a man
No one does what Albert can
They called him Albert Timmins

He blessed the humble on the street
Women swooned between his feet
This man named Albert Timmins

Flowers wilted when he passed
So great the shadow that he cast
That legend Albert Timmins
Lions calm beside him lay
When Albert turned night into day
Such was the fire in Albert Timmins

Mothers' sons were oft beseeched
If Albert's stature could be reached
"Oh please become like Albert!"
Wives wished husbands had the knack
To be like Albert in the sack
To love like Albert Timmins

He rode on horseback mighty fine
Turned plain water into wine
This man named Albert Timmins
Soldiers off to battle fled
When Albert lit the path ahead
Onward march with Albert Timmins

"Forward," rang his battle call
Alas the hero had to fall
"What ails you, Albert Timmins?"
And all around they wail and cry
As they watch magnificence die
Our hero, Albert Timmins.

They called him Albert Timmins
They called him Albert Timmins

The End.

Holly places the pencil in a tin, smiles at the teacher, walks out of the classroom without saying goodbye.

When she's been missing a month, the teacher offers Holly's song to the police, her soft smudged writing like spiders' legs marching across the page.

They search between the words, to see if there are any clues.

But all they find is a song about a villain, written by a girl who made him good. A girl who danced like a silverfish.

The Vacation That Never Was

She went to South Korea, to find her *aegyo* face.

Minnie's husband found her cute, but reading the spaces between Albert's wistful sighs, she felt he would prefer her cuter still.

Living in the shadow of wives one and two, and the wake of many others, Minnie worked hard to please him. She was a wizard in the kitchen and a genie in the bedroom. And still he wanted her eyes a little wider, her voice apple-sweet.

Albert said he'd take her for a surgical vacation, so she could be fixed.

In Seoul, he showed her places he'd visited in his youth. He took her to the Changdeokgung, and she broke a kitten-heel walking through the gardens surrounding the palace.

He told her about the Miracle on the Han River, filling her cup with soju. Told her how South Korea was transformed, and she would be too.

"Maybe I shouldn't drink any more," Minnie said, placing her palm over the glass, her leaf-like hand a statement that could not be ignored. She thought she'd best stay sober before facing the surgeon's knife.

They'd talked about eyelid surgery, but settled on some tightening on her forehead and a vaginoplasty.

"Next time," she'd said, "I'll have a tummy tuck, and something done to my bottom."

"Next time," Albert had said, as if she were a child, and could not be trusted to hold all her toys at once.

Mary Mary

They don't listen to me when I tell them I loved her. The skin on my wrists is twisted and sore. The skin on hers is red and blistered.

"Follow me, sir," the shorter one says. I don't want to go.

I can't leave Mary.

My fifth wife is petite, not much more than a child. Mary likes roses. She doesn't like spiders. She once cut her hair and gave it to a friend with stones for eyes. She shuns violence, appreciates kindness shown to her. She despises people who lie.

She loved me as no other ever has.

Mary bought a porcelain animal after every miscarriage. She gave each one the name we would have given our child.

Wilfred

Wendy

Wayne

Waveney

Walter

They never found a reason why our children withered and died before they were born. After the first two, Mary collected the *products of conception* and submitted them for analysis. I have my own ideas. I can guess why they weren't viable. I keep those thoughts to myself now, as I did then.

"Oh, Albert," she'd cry, stroking the latest ceramic addition.

I would wipe her tears with the back of my hand.

The last things I glimpse as they lead me away are her silent tears. Though stilled in death, the tears are not yet dry on her swollen face, as if even now, she's asking why.

Blue Notes

There are things my wife will never find out about, though sometimes I think Michelle knows what happens, but doesn't acknowledge it, if you see what I mean. After all, that leather jacket she's wearing didn't come cheap. It's not the colour I would have chosen, clashes with the yellow of her hair. But as long as the gifts keep coming, she'll overlook my indiscretions, as I do hers.

"And Albert." She leans against the doorjamb. "Don't forget to feed Pike and Prudence. Oh and Semi called."

I'm sitting in the lounge, picking goo from under my nails, wearing only my Marks and Spencer underpants. "Will do," I shout to her retreating back. "What did Semi want?"

"Call him," she says and the door clicks.

I wait for the clack of her shoes down the stairs, and the crunch of the front door. As soon as she's gone, I pull on a fresh pair of trousers, push some gel through what little hair I have, choose the grey shirt, no the check one, and call Semi while tipping biscuits out for the animals. There's no reply. Pike and Prudence chow down the food like they've reached cat heaven.

Jazzy lives on the other side of town. It takes almost an hour to drive there. When I arrive, she's projecting scenes of a swirling ocean onto the giant screen that fills half the wall. The soundtrack comes from boxy speakers on either side of a galley of recording equipment. It's her voice, yet it's not her voice, and there's the roar of waves, the chime of prayer bells like falling coins. Her hands are on her guitar, coaxing sounds from the instrument. Her hands are on my hands, her head close to mine.

She lives with the stars
He dies with the moon
Her true voice is swallowed in our kiss.

"Can you stay the night?" She pulls away and turns in time to the music, polarising me. I want to watch her dance. I want to take her away from the sound of her own voice. The white waves beat onto the shore on her wall. Everything is an illusion.

One more kiss.

When we kiss again, I want to stay in her music, but inevitably we don't.

Later I tell her it won't be long. She comments about my loveless marriage. The ocean beats in time to the rhythm of her voice.

Alone forever.

In the car I flick through my phone messages. There's one from Semi.

They're all gone.

That's all he says. I don't message him back. I don't call. I don't need to ask who *they* are, and where they have gone.

I drive back to my wife in sombre mood.

Pike sits on Michelle's knee like a cushion. I can tell from the timbre of her voice she's been crying.

"Semi rang," she says, nuzzling the creature. She looks like she might strangle it.

"He sent me a message, but I wasn't sure what it meant." I sling my jacket over a chair. "Something about them all being gone."

"His whole family," Michelle says. "They took the building out. They never stood a chance."

Semi's been trying to bring them over here for more than a year. He won't need to anymore.

And all I hear are the words of Jazzy's song.

Alone forever.

Dancing with Three Left Feet

The horses have been well cared for, though one has a fresh scar on the poll, just behind the left ear. Some are likely not as young as Kent Traminer says, but Hector takes them anyway. None have the sheen and stature of Shi Yin, Albert Timmins' horse in the next stall. But it's said Albert gave his soul away to have that horse. It's said he made a pact with a God from a far away land. Some say Albert Timmins is a God himself. But Hector thinks there's no harm in the man. If Timmins is a God, he's a benign deity. All the same, Hector would love to ride Shi Yin almost as much as he would like to court Beth Bellinger. But doesn't every man in the parish under the age of thirty feel that way about Beth?

Hector leans over the fence, looks again at the magnificent beast. Shi Yin blows a little hot air through her nostrils. Something drops from the brim of his hat onto his cheek. Hector freezes. He knows what it is. A cold sweat runs down his back, and his hands lock, the right resting over his holster.

"Hector Price!" A man's voice cracks the air. He mustn't show his fear. Brushing the offending creature from his chest, he turns to greet Albert Timmins. Hector forces a tight smile. He's aware the creature is still on his body. The size of a thumbnail, the spider drops to his boot, and then scuttles away. It has a peculiar walk, three left feet to five on the right. Hector cannot abide spiders, but something prevents him from squashing the life from it with the toe of his boot.

"You'll be coming to the dance tonight," Hector says, walking towards Timmins. Beth Bellinger alights from her father's carriage on the other side of the street. Both men turn to look at her.

"Yes. Me and my cousin Ben," Albert says.

Hector nods. Ben is an agile dancer, full of grace. It's not only a dance Hector is hosting, it is a contest too. Like one of Dmitri Yelchin's cockfights, Hector knows all but the winner will leave battered and bruised.

They take turns dancing with Beth Bellinger, cavorting to the sound of fiddles and harmonicas. She is as pretty as a pearl. Kent Traminer asks for the first dance. Beth is nimble on her feet. Old Man Bellinger watches carefully. His daughter will make her choice tonight. Beth's father has scrutinised all possible matches. Beth will not dance with anyone he has not approved.

Herman Schill exudes elegance, when he steps to the floor with Beth. And though he waltzes like a dream, all present know Beth will not select him, because who would choose a man who doesn't want to be chosen?

When Hector's turn comes, he steps in time to the music. A flash of invisible fire passes between them when he takes Beth's hand. Back, forth, back, forth, step, two three, back, two three. Hector is glad he practiced the moves with his sister. Timmins and Traminer watch with envy in their eyes. They'll know that Hector's performance surpasses theirs. Timmins may be a God, but he's no dancer.

And then he sees them. Not one, but two black creatures drop from Albert Timmins' hand to the floor. At that moment, Hector freezes, almost loses his footing. Kent Traminer steps forward and squashes one of the spiders, leaving a brown stain. The other has disappeared. Hector doesn't know where.

He takes several beats to right himself, to erase the fear, to re-apply the smile, to give everything he has to this dance. For a moment, he dances with three left feet. For a moment, he is unable to remember the steps to this dance that will determine his future. And Beth's. But the moment passes, and he finishes with an elegance that wins a smile from the girl.

Hector bows to Papa Bellinger, returns his daughter to him. For the moment.

Albert Timmins' cousin Ben steps forward to ask Beth to join him on the floor. Hector knows the musicians are tired. They have played their fiddles with burning fingers. The accordion player sips his ale. The dance is almost over. Ben whispers into the man's ear, and the musician nods.

When Ben takes Beth's hand, there is lightness in his steps, flight in his movement. There is something in the way the young couple move around each other, as if they have danced tarantella all their lives.

At that moment Hector realises he has done well enough, but Ben has *surpassed* him, and Beth is lost forever.

Comfort Women

The smell of urine and desperation.

The fire in empty eyes.

This small room with its bamboo walls, its malarial air, with the echo of death in its doorways. This room, where I have heard a thousand cries.

Her face is small and round and sad.

Many of the women who work here come from Korea. Some are Japanese, others Dutch, and a few Indonesian. They wear a badge of despair. There is something in their eyes. Something in the way they hold themselves.

She knows I am a prisoner. I am like her. She knows I'm not here to use her services. She knows I have no voucher. I have nothing to give her in exchange for what she can offer. She knows she may not eat tonight, if she does not work, for where have the soldiers gone?

"It's over," I say, my voice a whisper. I can hardly believe my own words. "Perhaps you can go home now?"

"I take care," she says, removing her robe. "Care you." Perhaps she has misunderstood after all.

"No," I raise my hand. "No. That's not why I'm here."

There's a cry outside. I tense and then relax when I hear the accented words.

"It's over!"

More cries.

Has it really been twenty-seven years? Another ending. Another Armistice. We thought it could never happen again. Yet it did.

How many more times?

Exultant cries.

Defiant cries.

She looks at me, uncertain. I find the cigarettes I stole from a dying man earlier that evening.

She reaches for the matches on the table and lights me up. We smile at each other. I suck in the cool blue smoke, and pass it to her. Her fingers are damp, like everything else in this place.

"My name is Albert." I point to my chest.

"Albert," she repeats.

"And you?"

"You?" she asks.

"Your name?" I take the cigarette back.

"My name?" She looks down towards her feet. "Rina."

"A pleasure to meet you, Rina."

We talk. We smoke. The sun goes down like a bomb, and we are engulfed in darkness, the only light comes from the tip of the next cigarette.

We talk. She finds the lamp with her fingers. They brush against my waist on the way. We talk a little longer in its orange-yellow glow. I wonder what will happen next, how I shall get out of this place. How I'll get back home.

She speaks about a little boy, a mother, a father. A husband. Perhaps they are all dead, she says.

"Don't give up hope," I tell her, though I know I'm speaking to myself as well.

"There is a stone in my heart," she says. A tear forms, and I wipe it away with my thumb.

"There is a diamond in your heart," I tell her.

They burst through the door. Their shouts are like summer garlands. One of the soldiers takes her hands, and they dance in a circle of joy.

I catch Rina's eye.

I'm not sure if she knows whether to laugh or cry.

Cruise

Albert complains when I wear yellow. Says it clashes with me hair. He's one to talk. He don't take much care about what he wears under that robe of his. Like them disciples, as he calls 'em don't notice his ten year old Adidas T-shirt, black stripes showing when he lifts his arms to do them yogic postures. I aren't exaggeratin' when I says it's buggered.

And don't get me started on the underpants.

"You need to be careful," I says to him. "Them so called disciples of yours, they're our bread and butter."

"How do you mean, careful?"

"They'll see you for what you are, if you don't keep up the mystical mumbo jumbo. They don't expect their guru to wear Nike trainers and to put a tenner on the horses for the Grand National."

"What they won't know won't hurt them."

"Mark my words, the real you shows through more than you know." I cross me arms, but have to re-adjust the bikini. Ever since the second boob job, me bosoms have been like Houdini, escapin' at the drop of a hat.

"Do you think you know the real me, Michelle?" Albert gives me that smile. The one that makes him look like a snake. "Do you think you know who I *really* am?"

"I know you better than anyone else does," I says, and smear sun cream on his shoulders.

"Really? If you knew me that well, you'd know I can't stand you wearing yellow."

Oh I know that all right. But it's not the yellow this time, I reckon. It's the bikini itself. It's the looks I'm getting from men a lot younger than Albert Timmins. They gawp at me when they stroll along the deck. Me skin flecked with sequins of water from me last dip in the pool, I don't look bad for me age. I make sure I keep me hair dry. So it stays *yellow*.

121

I wear yellow to dinner. There're three shops on the boat that sell clothes at three times the price you pays at Marks and Spencer. I got meself a lovely sunflower-bright number. And matching earrings. The sea's a bit rough tonight, and I don't much feel like eatin' me supper. Don't want to gip on me new frock.

"When's the first time you ever went on a ship?" I ask Albert, and lick the juice off of a prawn.

"Ever?"

"Ever."

"1756."

"No, I mean *when* was the first time, Albert." I mop me lips with a serviette. "And I dunno where seventeen fifty-whatever is. Is that a port from your army days?"

He gives me this eerie look. It's not the snake smile this time. This one's worse than the snake lips.

"I mean the year, seventeen fifty-six."

"Yeah right." I snort a little laugh. But when Albert doesn't laugh back, I realise what he said ain't funny. And somehow I don't think it's the rockin' of the boat that's makin' me feel queasy.

It's somethin' else altogether.

Apple

in finding divine mysteries and universal meaning Albert Timmins disámbiguates the lessons of his Holy Father although it is a little known fact that there are not one but three original men at the beginning of the world and of course a whole load of women who become mothers of the men and each other through some awkwardly inept form of parthenogenesis which Albert finds unpretentious and confusing at the same time because there are his sons who are also his fathers there is Ra who shines like liniment and has a crooked smile which can down the moon but he is less effective than his brother who is made from both fire and soil and both his sisters who calm the lost souls impatient to be born and his sun-father Xavier who is the apple of the abdomen of his Holy mother

Dmitri's Leg

Nobody knows how old Dmitri Yelchin is. I'd be surprised if he knew himself. No one knows how he came to have a withered leg. It hangs limply from his hip, and no one knows whether he will ever walk again.

Old Man Bellinger has taken pity on the farm hand. He allows Dmitri to sleep in a cot next to the late Mrs. Bellinger's saddles and boots in the lower part of the house, not far from the stables.

The woman who takes care of the cows feeds the sick man with a long-handled wooden spoon. Mabel won't take him to the latrines though. I've heard that is left to the young stable boy, though the odour suggests he doesn't always do his duty on time. The boy is the same one who is looking after Old Dmitri's birds so they don't die. The only time those birds are allowed to die is when Dmitri puts them in the arena. Birds often perish in their work. That's the way with cock fighting.

I have brought my horse Shi Yin for new shoes. Bellinger's blacksmith is the best. I will use no other.

"Ah, Albert Timmins," Old Man Bellinger calls when he walks past the forge and sees me. "You're having your horse shod?"

"I am."

"Call into the house while you wait. Perhaps Mabel will fetch you a glass of porter." He heads towards his carriage.

"I will."

That is how I come to spy young Beth Bellinger talking to Dmitri when I enter the house through the rear entrance. The door to the old man's makeshift infirmary is open a few inches. I see the cream lace of her dress through the space between door and frame. The honey of her voice melts something in my chest, so I stop to listen for a while. It's not that I want to pry, only that I rarely have the opportunity to hear the music of Beth's words.

"What shall I bring you?" Bellinger's daughter asks the old man.

"Whiskey." Dmitri's voice is hoarse, stricken with thirst and illness. "I'm so parched, I could bite into my flesh and drink my own blood."

"I cannot give you whiskey," says Beth. I pull nearer to the door.

"Water," he gasps.

"The water from the well is not sweet."

I try not to push the door any wider when I draw closer. They must not know I am here.

"Wine," he croaks.

Beth Bellinger leans over him. Her fingers are close to his throat.

"You know I cannot give you wine." Her voice is sugar-sweet as she reaches into the purse he wears on a leather cord around his neck. "The wine is too strong." Her hands come away from the purse. "Tell me once more what you would like to drink." The glint of gold is an accusation in her fingers.

"Warm milk." The man spits the words out. "When I drink from your cup, I'll know I am truly loved."

Beth slips away without answering. She has what she wants. I feign surprise at seeing her in the lower house when I step inside.

No one knows how long Dmitri has lived in these parts. No one knows where he came from. Poor Dmitri dancing between dreams and desire. Dmitri with his withered leg and feckless birds, Dmitri, who has never known love.

Nobody knows where he will go from here.

I fear it will be the grave.

Mary

The skin on my wrist is twisted; the skin on hers blistered.
    "Follow me," someone says. I don't want to leave Mary.

My wife is petite, little more than a child. She liked roses, despised spiders. She gave her hair to her friend Salma, who has eyes of stone.
    Mary despised people who lie.
    She loved me as no other ever has.

Mary bought porcelain after every miscarriage. Our children withered and died before they were born. I had my ideas why, but I kept those thoughts to myself.
    "Oh, Albert," she'd cry.
    I would wipe her tears away.

I glimpse her silent tears stilled in death.
    Even now, she's asking why.

Comfort Girl

Look, there's no point beating around the bush, and beating off doesn't cut the mustard, but in times like these, you can't beat the love of a good woman.

I know where to go. Wrap brown paper around my head, leaving a hole I can see out of. It's not much of a filter to breathe through, and my lungs won't thank me, but paper's all I've got, and I'm lucky to have that.

Much of the walk to the red-light district is uphill. I'll appreciate coming down the hill afterwards, in more ways than one.

Don't know why we call these places red-light zones anymore. There is nothing red about them, and there's certainly not much light around. It's a throwback from an earlier time, I suppose.

The women occupy what's left of some of the finer homes in the district. The buildings will have been magnificent once, with indoor pools, and ventilated bunkers. Fat lot of good either did for the former occupants.

The hallway smells of urine and desperation.

The minder examines my payment.

"Can't eat that," he says tossing aside Michelle's yellow jacket. Sacrilege. If only he knew how hard it had been for me to keep hold of that all these years. Mary's ring is treated with the same contempt. I make sure I retrieve them, put the jacket in my pack, the ring back on my finger. Eventually he settles for a lump of dried pork. At least I tell him the meat is pork.

A woman with black curtains of hair passes between us. Her eyes are covered with membranes of disease and distrust.

"I would let you have Salma," he says, "but she has other duties." He slaps Salma's backside. The woman's wig looks like it could have been woven from my former wife's hair. Salma gives the minder a stony look, and I want to stroke her head.

The girl he offers me has glittery spangles on her dress, and is jittery in her movements. Her candle gutters and spits, making the shadows in the room dance.

She knows I am a prisoner. In many ways, I am just like her.

"What's your name?" I ask as the door closes.

"Today, it's Sonja," she says, and leads me to the rude cot in the middle of the room. Her wrists are slick with perfumed oils, and I am reminded of another girl, another time. Sonja rubs the back of my neck, and brings her hands lower, moving them faster, as she has been taught.

I am seized with a melancholic desire not to hurt her.

"Can we slow things down?"

"We don't have much time, Mister."

"Albert. Call me Albert," I insist.

Sonja brushes the hair from her eyes, opens her robe to reveal plumb-tight breasts.

"Let's talk a while," I try, but her head is already between my thighs. And well, you can lead a horse away from water, but this horse needs to drink.

Afterwards Sonja tidies away the petals she's strewn beneath us. She hands me the tattered pieces of paper, the scattered clothing. I fumble with my pants. She hurries me with her eyes. I mumble about the difficulties of arthritis.

"Here, let me help," she says.

"Are you happy in this place?" I ask. It is a pointless question. The answer lies in the situation. In the surroundings, the dull ache of her eyes.

"Are any of us happy, wherever we are?"

"Come away with me." I take her hand.

She laughs, a metallic, empty sound.

"Well?" I ask, wondering how I would feed her.

"You're not the first to ask." She shakes her head.

"And?"

"And what?" Her voice is kind, but hurried.

"Why did they change their minds?"

"How do you know they changed their minds, Albert?" Sonja passes me my shoes. There is a hole in the bottom of the right. I hope the walk back is less arduous than the climb here.

"You're still here, aren't you? That's how."

"And you imagine that's a bad thing."

"How old are you, Sonja?"

"Old enough."

"What year were you born?"

She hesitates, as if subtracting. "Twenty seventy-five."

She cannot really be sixteen years old.

There was a time I would have gone to prison for what I have just done, but no one cares anymore.

No one cares in twenty ninety-one.

So long as they are paid well enough, with something they can eat.

Bombs

Come away from the bombs
Find a new life
Safety our first priority
Must be able to swim

His Yemeni name is Shamir. It means flint. But the people in the hosiery factory reckon they can't say that, so they call him Semi.

I bring him a cup of tea, because that's what you do.

"Thank you, Albert." Semi takes the cup with trembling hands. His accent is less pronounced than when I first met him.

He used to call me *Thakur Baba* back then, though Semi wasn't one of my disciples. He's never been that stupid. He answered the advert I put in the local supermarket for a cleaner. The studio gets awfully dirty after my hot-hot yoga sessions, especially when someone passes out.

Michelle refused to do it after Tony the Twat collapsed and sliced his scalp on the radiator. There was a lot of blood. Gormless Goral made it worse when he tried to give Tony the kiss of life. He'd focussed more on the kiss part than the chest compressions, and had to be pulled away. The Twat hadn't even needed resuscitating and had come round by then anyway. There was blood all over the parquet. My wife informed me she wasn't going to touch any of it, so I had to clean it myself.

That's how Semi came into our lives. He was the only one willing to work for the pittance I offered. Of course I have increased his pay several times since then. I like the guy. And we can afford it. God knows, Michelle and I can't keep up with the demand from the millennials and tofu munchers who come to *Thakur Baba* for enlightenment. They want to find themselves. They have discovered the route through me championing humanitarian ideals, freedom of

130

thought, and other phrases I find from my Hare Krishna free books and the Bertrand Russell Wikipedia page.

All the other applicants had laughed when I mentioned the hourly rate, despite the promise of being seeped in wondrous knowledge through proximity to *Thakur Baba.*

"Do you remember the advertisement you placed in the shop?" Semi sips tea and grimaces. His English is overly perfect in a way a native speaker's never is. He wants to talk about other things. Anything apart from the grief that tears a hole the size of Somalia in his heart.

I'd placed the advert hoping to snare a student or someone else who knew no better:

Cleaner required
Thakur Baba's hot-hot yoga studio
Find enlightenment through the back door
Must have floor buffing experience

"You were the best applicant," I tell Semi.

"That is not true." He smiles a knowing smile.

"And you'd never buffed a floor in your life."

"I didn't know what a buffing was!" It's good to hear him laugh.

I lift the plate of Rich Tea biscuits, wave them under his nose, but he raises his palm in refusal.

"What attracted you to the job? Surely not the promise of acquiring overt wisdom by nefarious means?" I try to use new words when talking to Semi. He laps them up.

"I needed the money." It's as simple as that. He needed a second job, even if the pay was scandalously low. "There is another advertisement I wish I had never answered." He pronounces it *advertise-ment* rather than *adver-tisement.*

"Oh?"

"When I left my country. I never should have come away without them. Should have been all of us, or none of us." And the dam breaks. I wish Michelle hadn't chosen to go shopping when she heard Semi was coming over. *I'll leave you boys to chat in private,* she'd said.

None of us like to deal with another's grief.

131

I clap my hand on Semi's back and squeeze his heaving shoulders.

"I escaped the bombs. I left my little boy, my mother, my father. My wife," he says.

After Semi leaves, I think of more words I will share with him. He'll be familiar with some of them. Others will be new.

Woe
Wanton
Wreckage
Waste
Wretchedness
Widower

The Original Thakur Baba

The steamy heat and unfulfilled promise of rain all but finished me off that summer. There wasn't an inch of skin untouched by mosquitoes. We spent a lot of the season waiting. Waiting in the sickly heat, being devoured by all of God's creatures that had a taste for human flesh. All I wanted was to go back home.

Despite my officer's training at the Company's military academy I had no appetite for fighting, and I'd long since forgotten why it was important for us to be there.

The sky was a thick grey that day, and threatened to crack with rain at any moment. I wanted to get away, if only for a short while.

I'd been chatting to one of the sepoys, a portly chap who kept his fingernails long, and his temper short. This fellow came from Oudh. He had a moustache that could have cut glass. He offered to take me to see a wise man he knew.

"Captain Timmins, this man is a god. He makes gold coins appear from thin air, and," he paused for effect, "he speaks in tongues."

I had nothing better to do that night, so I went with him. I thought it might cure my disinterested mood.

A platoon of dark boys were fanning themselves with leaves the size of dinner-plates as we left the compound. They complained lustily about weevils in the rice and a lack of clean water, as if we could do anything to help them.

We'd been warned against venturing into native territory on our own, and cautioned to stay in groups. Though there was only the two of us, I felt I was in safe hands with this chap. He knew the narrow alleys and steep pathways that led to poorly lit hovels where one could purchase tooth powder, abortifacients or lozenges to cure dropsy.

The illuminated entrance led to a room where they were burning gharuwood incense. The fellow sat on a dais. His hair was the colour of onions. His nose curved like a beak, his fingernails extended like claws. The violet smoke entered my body, making me cough. The sepoy, however, appeared to be immune.

They called the wise man Thakur Baba. An old fellow with snake-coiled hair collected coins from the crowd, while the fakir on the stage lifted a white-filmed mist from a woman's eye.

"I can see," the woman declared in her own tongue. And whilst I did not understand all her words without help from the native, it was abundantly clear what had occurred.

Thakur Baba cured a lame man of his palsy by feeding him the chalky white powder he pushed from the shaft of a peacock feather.

He turned foul water to sweet, pulled family jewels that had been lost for centuries from a woman's navel, and silenced the ensuing clamour of accusations with a click of his tongue.

I was familiar with sleight of hand from my days watching the ship's entertainer on the long voyage out. I slipped away from the crowd while my companion had a gilt button pulled from his ear.

Capable of a little trickery myself, I crept into the rooms at the back of the hovel, stepping from one to another, slipping items of value into my pocket: a gentleman's fob watch and a set of dice, though I left the curved cutlass I desired, unable to conceal it in my clothing.

It was in the very last chamber that I came upon a shell of a woman curled on a charpoy, emaciated, with translucent skin and hooded eyes.

"Who goes there," she cried.

I stepped into the light of her candle, gave a false name, rank and regiment, my words slow and stilted in the native language.

"What is your business here?"

"I'm seeking rebels," I lied. For though I, Albert Timmins, was little more than a common thief, I played the part of someone with a righteous purpose.

"Who are you?" I asked in broken Hindustani, maintaining the moral authority that came with my position. I would be asking the questions, not she.

"I am Roma," the woman said. "They are trying to kill me," she added, imploring me to take her away in order to save her life. The sound of the crowd in the antechamber filtered through. No doubt Thakur Baba had performed another miraculous feat.

"Who wishes to harm you," I asked, my curiosity piqued. "And are you not free to leave of your own volition?"

Roma pulled the ragged blanket away from her wasted legs to reveal the shackles that held her in position. "My sons," she continued. It took me a moment to understand what she was accusing her own flesh and blood of.

"Your sons did this?" I checked we were alone. Her shins were so thin they could almost have slipped through the ankle cuffs.

"That charlatan taking coins from gullible people," Roma continued, "is my younger son." She was referring to snake hair. "And the Baba is the elder."

"Where is the key?" I asked.

"It is tucked in Thakur Baba's clothing." She spat the name out like poison. "You will have to find another way."

I manipulated the lock with the tip of my dagger with little effect.

"This house is mine," she spoke as I worked. "It has been in my family for generations."

Another roar came from the crowd, tumultuous and rapturous.

"They want my property. They did this when I tried to stop their exploitation."

I heard footsteps.

I was about to abandon her to her fate when the lock sprang open.

"You are a god, my son," Roma called to my retreating back. "You are a god, gracious and noble, Albert Timmins."

I left her to make her own escape, and joined the sepoy in the audience, wondering how she knew my name, when I'd never told her.

No Comfort in February

Shi Yin is weary, and I am exhausted beyond measure. It's been a long day. I have toiled in the sun. After checking the ostler will see to my horse's needs, I trudge up the steps and enter Molly Flanagan's emporium.

Mrs. Yelchin behind the bar greets me with her coarse voice, pours a whiskey that disappears before she gives me my change. I take the coins and ask for more liquor.

A gathering of farmhands sits on the far side of the inn. Robert Worsley is amongst them. The others I don't know. I tip my hat in their direction, but don't join them. The men laugh, tell bawdy jokes and slap their thighs in time to the piano. Old Wellard beats out a melody on the cracked and crusted keys. The joanna is out of tune, and could do with a good seeing to.

It's not clear whether Worsley and his friends are drinking before availing themselves of Molly's ladies. There are many girls to choose from, more since the traders passed this way. None satisfy my thirst for a woman though, as much as the dark-skinned girl called February.

"We're ready for you, Albert," Molly says, gesturing towards the stairs. "February will see you next." I hadn't noticed Molly enter the salon. I drain my drink and follow her up the stairs. Two girls in frothy dresses lean against the railings, smiling at me, tilting their heads sideways and back and sideways again, as if their posturing might persuade me to spend my hard earned wages on them instead.

Molly licks her finger before counting the notes. She whistles when she see's how much I have given her.

"You wantin' to pay for a month, Mr. Albert?"

"I want to stay the night," I tell her, indicating the case by my side.

Molly scratches her head. Her perfumed silver curls toss like meadow flowers. "That would be most irregular."

"This is a hotel, isn't it? That's what the sign says."

"Sure it's a hotel." She rolls up half the bills and hands them back to me. "So will you be dining with us?"

"Yes Ma'am. And I'd like Miss February to join me."

"She's working, Albert. You know that. Every night 'cept Mondays."

"Yes, I know." I push the money back into Molly's fat pink hand. "And I would like to spend the evening, and the night with her."

Molly counts the notes again. "It's going to cost you much more than what you have here, Albert Timmins."

"You drive a hard bargain, Mrs. Flanagan."

I count out more notes until she is satisfied, and tell her I'll meet February in the dining hall at eight o'clock. I ask if she will kindly show me to my room.

"Your room?" Molly asks.

"Why, yes. You said this is a hotel. Please show me to my room." She is flustered for a moment, instructs me to wait in the salon, and asks one of the girls in bubbling lace to fetch fresh sheets for my room.

"I ain't no chamber maid," a girl hollers as I clamber down the stairs.

"You think you're too good to strip a bed, May Fox?" Molly continues.

"Yes Ma'am. I am."

"But you're not too grand to strip down to your drawers on a bed, and — "

I don't hear the rest, because I'm asking Mrs. Yelchin to pour me another drink. I enquire after her husband. She tells me Dmitri is no better, but that someone has robbed him whilst he lay in his sickbed. She uses the corner of her dishcloth to mop a tear from her eye. We curse at the brazen behaviour of the thief.

"And his birds have taken ill too," she adds, confirming my suspicions that the stable boy charged with caring for Dmitri Yelchin's fighting birds is himself under the influence of Yelchin's rivals.

At eight o'clock precisely, February Begaye enters the dining room and I pull her chair out. The candles make her hair gleam like polished wood. Though it is braided, the sheer bulk of it speaks of opulence. I ask what she would like.

"A little broth," she says. "Nothing more." Her downcast eyes are coal-black and honest.

"Just for tonight, you understand," I say, before I even open the box. "It's a game I want to play, nothing more." I place the ring that was to have been Beth Bellinger's on February's finger. Her hands are small, so it goes on her middle digit. It is the very size of her that makes February my favourite. "Just for tonight," I repeat, so there can be no misunderstanding, "I wish you to be Mrs. Timmins."

"For tonight," she repeats. After a moment's hesitation, she twists the ring, admires it, and slips into the role.

"How was your day on the farm, dearest?"

I speak of my travails. She listens.

"And our sons," she asks. "Tell me how they fared."

"Wesley works hard." I imagine a boy, wide-shouldered with his mother's bronze skin.

"He does," she says. "So does his brother. How is Walter? Always wanting to stand tall with the grown men, yet not strong enough to chop firewood for me." February brings the spoon to her lips.

"Wilhelmina chides her brother so," I continue, enjoying the game.

"Albert," she asks finally.

"Yes?"

"What is it that makes a man wise?"

"A man must know the purpose of his movements and be aware of his place in the universe."

After dining, we retire. Mrs. Timmins snuffs the lantern and lies in my arms. Though I feel a stirring in my loins, I will not defile this sacred hour. I hold her with longing. I hold her with love, and think of what might have been.

For at that moment, the woman in my arms is Beth, and it is then that I find no comfort in February.

Crab

Minnie asks me to polish the wine glasses, and I oblige. Afterwards, I turn the cricket on and sip my beer. She comes into the lounge and pouts.

"What?" I ask.

"I need help. They'll be here soon."

"But I did what you asked, honey."

"Can you lay the cutlery out?" Her inflated lips sit like tulip petals on her petite face.

"I guess." I turn the television louder, so I can keep up with the score.

"And can you fetch a knitting needle from my craft box?"

"Knitting needle?" I ask, turning at the kitchen door.

"Preferably a size eight or nine, if you can find one," she yells from the kitchen. "Do you know where to find them, Albert?"

"I think so."

When I return, I pause to look at my wife. She's doing something with the crabs. One of them moves a claw lazily. Water bubbles in a pot on the stove. It sounds like rain. When Minnie turns and scuttles to the fridge, I take in the oversized bow in her hair, the polka dots, and the breasts that look like they were plucked from a larger woman and edited onto her. She looks like someone who threw away the book of her life and rewrote herself.

And I have helped.

"I have the needle." I twirl it like a conductor's baton.

"It goes on the right. Outside the smallest knife."

"Huh?"

"For Deborah," she says, as if that explains why we need a small metal spike on the dining table.

"For Deborah?" If I keep repeating what she says, maybe it will begin to make sense.

"Deborah likes to eat crab with a knitting needle."

139

What the jolly fuck?

After our guests leave, I stack the dishes, wipe the knitting needles dry before returning them where I found them. Turns out Wyatt wanted one too, so I brought a whole bunch to the table, sizes eight, nine and ten, and a crochet hook for good measure. We used them to poke the flesh from the crabs' legs and claws, splashed each other with marine flesh.

Minnie lounges on the sofa. She's had a little too much wine. Her speech is slurred, her hair wilting. Her make-up turns her into a Picasso painting. There's something on the tellie about the first Buddha.

"That bitch called again," she says between hiccups. "Did you know?"

How would I know, if she didn't tell me? By *that bitch*, I can only assume she means Michelle.

– *the first Buddha was moved by the innate suffering of humanity* –

Some wives have cordial relations with their partner's ex-wives. This is not the case between Minnie and Michelle, even though it's two years since I left my former wife. I left her for Minnie in the winter of 2018. Two years of screaming on the phone, rocks thrown at our windows (or *her* windows, as Michelle likes to call them). Two years of near financial ruin, my secrets exposed, broadcast, my weaknesses made public on Facebook and other social media. It nearly finished me.

"What did she want?" I am careful not to fuel Minnie's anger.

– *and its endless repetition is due to rebirth* –

"I don't know." She stretches a leg out on the sofa, raises the ankle onto the armrest. It looks swollen. There is a ladder running through her stocking.

– *insight into the workings of karma and his former lives* –

She threatens to expose the tops of her hosiery when she twists for the TV remote, her pleated mini-skirt falling around her thighs like a deck if cards.

"I'll call her in the morning," I say, watching a game show contestant collapse in tears.

"Don't call her at all," Minnie says. The cute *aegyo* face contorts into angry-little-girl mode, like someone threw her into a fire, and she started to melt.

Michelle might be trying to contact me about something important, something to do with lawyers and family trusts. But I'm not prepared to have her shout at me for waking her at an ungodly hour. So I reassure Minnie.

"You're right." I scratch my ear. "Best let sleeping dogs lie."

"Are you calling that woman a dog?"

Seems I can't win. Minnie had referred to her as a *bitch* herself.

"I didn't mean anything by it."

"She's not good enough to be a dog," Minnie says, and burps angrily.

I catch the faint whiff of crab on her breath.

Raft of Bones

It is said human beings came out of Africa, but I was there when we went *in*, and I know things are not as they seem. Holy books, historians and scientists make me laugh with their wild theories and assumptions.

I've seen Ra, Xavier and others who marched in time to the crashing light at the beginning. I knew Alissandre, who kept the bones of his lovers to build a raft, to fulfil his dreams of escape.

And of course there's me, Albert Timmins, the primordial historian who saw everything.

The Boat

When the ferry pulls away from the harbour, Dad takes us to the top deck. I don't know where Mum is. The waves buck and rage against the side of the vessel. Dad pulls me back from the railings.

"Don't lean out. You'll fall in."

"I *won't*," I say, but don't disobey my father.

My sister runs the full length of the deck and back, and away again, until she's out of breath. She stops for air and collapses on the bench beside our father, breathing like a dog with heatstroke.

Mum appears with our little brother. Something clinks in her handbag. The gunfire burst of our brother's cries cracks the air. The wind squirrels through, blowing hair horizontal and sending scarves into water.

"Here," Mum says, and hands us a bottle of Bitter Lemon. "It's for you to share." There's another bottle for her and Dad. The drink hisses when I twist the cap off. Mum has brought paper cups, so my sister and I don't have to share sticky saliva on the bottle's lip. My brother sips greedily from Mum's cup. He leaves an imprint of crumbs on the rim.

The waves lift us higher and drop us down. My brother says he wants to pee. He wants to pee now. Right now. Mum takes the top off an empty Bitter Lemon bottle, points my brother's tiny penis into the lip, and collects the straw-coloured liquid. When he finishes, she caps the urine and tosses it out to sea, where it may lie for a hundred years. Fish will dance in curious circles around my brother's wee.

Years later, my sister will toss a whiskey bottle overboard from another boat, and I will remember this moment.

When the first drops of rain pelt our skins, we trickle down the stairways with hundreds of others and head for a lounge on a lower deck. The sun shines. A half-light illuminates the rain. I look for rainbows and find only the slivered sixpence of a morning moon.

The boy is crying again, so Mum takes him to the fruit machines at the far end of the lounge. Dad lights up a cigarette, and I luxuriate in the woody scent of blue smoke curling upwards.

"Do you want to try?"

I scrutinise my father's face for a smile, try to find the joke in his eyes, but he is deadly serious. My sister giggles.

"No," he says. "I mean it."

I look at my sister. She looks at me. We're both wearing party dresses for the holidays. Neither of us knows what to say.

"A cigarette is nothing special," Dad says. "You don't have to try them with your friends. Here, look. It's nothing." He passes the smoke to my sister first because she's older. She holds it like a piece of glass, like she's scared she will break it. She doesn't cough, but when it's my turn, I do.

"See now," he says. "You don't need to smoke again. It's bad for your health." The cool burn of minty smoke stays with me. I think it will stay for a hundred years. Mum likes Dad to smoke *Consulate*. She reckons mentholated cigarettes are safer, because they're only mint. She'll even share one with Dad occasionally. She's let me use some of her turquoise eye shadow today, because it's a holiday, and the normal rules don't apply.

The boat tosses and dips. It pitches and yaws. The lady in the next bay yelps. I slip from my parents' watchful gaze, find the fruit machines and drop a penny into the slot. I'm allowed one coin, because my brother was given one. I watch my penny disappear and am shocked by the intensity of my regret.

I will smoke again. I'll form a habit that lasts for years. But I'll never gamble. I'm distraught at the loss of my money, but I don't follow my first impulse to rush to my parents and beg for another penny.

I'm not allowed on any of the outdoor decks without the adults, but there is an open viewing port near the stairway. It's indoors and outdoors. You can feel the rush of the wind and imagine the spray when you climb onto the bottom railing. It is safe, though there is a scent of danger.

"What's your name?" the sailor says. His uniform is crisp white. There are bands on his shoulder. I say nothing. "This is a good place to look out from," he continues when I don't reply. "I'm Tim." I turn to look at him, count the buttons on his shirt. That's when he puts his arm around me, and I think it must be the turquoise eye shadow that's done it. I don't know whether I want to rub it off my face, or if I want to wear it forever. This is what it must be like to be wild and free. His arm is warm, and I am appalled and excited at the same time. Tim must be a hundred years older than me, but I feel a tiny bit sad when he walks away.

The boat lurches again. Silver spray washes over the glass at the front. A woman cries for Jesus, Mary and her heavenly father, but I'm not scared. I can feel the warmth of Tim's arm on my shoulders, even though he's gone.

I walk through the restaurant. There's a woman wearing a yellow dress that clashes with the straw-colour of her hair.

"When's the first time you ever went on a ship, Albert?" she asks a man who's too old to be her husband. He must be a hundred years older than her. She picks a prawn from her plate and licks the juice off it.

When I find them again, all but one of my family is asleep, tired from the early morning start.

Pole

A thirty-eight millimetre set screw connector and a three metre metal conduit. Hager consults his list. A woman who can't control her cart knocks into him, and tuts as she pushes her way through the throng. Several bags of woodchip bounce on the spring-loaded base of the trolley. Hager wouldn't be surprised if she amputates someone's leg with her erratic manoeuvring.

Lines of DIY enthusiasts stream past in both directions. A man with llama-eyes knocks Hager on the shoulder and gives him an accusatory glare.

Fucker.

Where can he find a castor wheel with a bolt on plate? And what about a fifteen-centimetre lag bolt? There's no one to ask.

"Excuse me." A woman in a boiler suit weaves between shoppers with the precision of a bomb-disposal expert until she knocks an old guy's ankle and detonates a volley of apologies between them.

Hager passes a cluster of dark-suited men with beards. They wear hats, and are universally short. The tops of the hats reach no higher than his chin. They speak in a foreign tongue. Their tangled glossolalia means nothing to Hager until the oldest points to a high shelf and grunts, the universal language. Hager reaches for the canister, passes it to the man, and is rewarded with a smile that reveals a difficult life and poor dental hygiene.

In the basement, the sound of the drill is like music to Hager, though Dorothea isn't impressed.

Stop it, his wife mouths at the top of the steps. Doesn't she get that he's doing this for her? She gesticulates, urging him to stop, so he does.

"It's past nine-thirty," she says. "The neighbours will complain."

Fuck the neighbours, Hager thinks. This is about Dorothea.

She'd wanted a pole-dancing pole in the basement. But now he's installing it, she seems unsure, as if she doubts her cellulitis-ridden body will glide through the air like the girls on Instagram do.

"Come and watch a film before we go to bed," his wife says. "I have peanuts."

If Dorothea ate fewer peanuts, Hager thinks, perhaps she wouldn't need a dancing pole in the basement to exercise on, to lose the excess weight. If she ate fewer peanuts, she probably wouldn't fart in her sleep. He puts the drill down carefully on a piece of circular plywood, and trudges upstairs.

"What are we going to watch?" He stifles a sigh.

Dorothea grabs a bunch of DVDs from the end of the shelf and calls out the titles.

Wallace and Gromit
War of the Worlds
West Side Story
Whale Rider
Whistle Down the Wind

"Yes, that one," Hager interrupts. "I like old films."

"*Whistle Down the Wind?* Hmmm. Not sure," Dorothea says, and Hager wonders why she consulted him at all.

"I like it. Tremendous music," he says. "Isn't Haley Mills in it?"

"Yes."

"The guy pretends to be slow," Hager says, "and ends up trying to kill her?"

"No. That's *Twisted Nerve*. This is the one where the kids believe an escaped convict is Jesus."

"Oh yes." They watch the movie and eat peanuts.

Hager cries when the film ends. He sniffs and clears his throat, pretends he's starting with a cold, and something's got into his eye. Perhaps it's an eyelash, he tells his wife.

"It's a beautiful story," Dorothea says, wiping her eyes with a tissue. "A great actress."

"Fancy thinking an ordinary man was Christ though," Hager says. As he heads to the basement though, he thinks perhaps it's not so easy to know when you're *actually* in the presence of the Son of God.

147

Hager sands the pole by hand, first with the rough grade, then with the fine sandpaper. The shine comes up beautifully. It is an act of love.

He thinks about when he'd dropped in to Albert Timmins' place earlier that day to borrow the drill, and Timmins had talked about making sacrifices to achieve atonement. Hager hadn't any idea what that had to do with the price of sausages, and wasn't Albert doing very well teaching hot-hot yoga and mindfuck-ness or whatever it was to a bunch of Gen Y brats?

Jammy devil.

What reason did he have to go on about sacrifice? And didn't he have a woman on the side that Michelle didn't know about? And wasn't he about to take his wife on a cruise, Hager had asked. Of course, Timmins had replied. He'd stroked Pike, one of his poky-faced cats, and told Hager he was learning to read Aramaic.

"Is that a sort of candy-bar?" Hager had asked. "And why do you need to read them?"

Albert had shaken his head, looking at Hager like he was a moron, then handed him the drill.

Hager uses Albert's drill to make a hole in the cup-shaped p.v.c. cap that will have the bolt run through it. Then he passes a magnet along the drywall to identify where the joists are screwed in.

The *eeeee-eeeee-eeeee* of the drill is soothing. It makes him feel like he's in control.

eeeee-eeeee-eeeee

eeeee-eeeee-eeeee

And can he hear shouting over the sound of it?

"What the fuck are you doing?" Dorothea slams the drill from his hand and it jumps out of his grasp.

eeeee-eeeee-eeeee-kerthunk

Albert's drill skids to a halt and bites into Hager's boot. There's a smell in the air, and the pain, the pain.

What has she done?

Dorothea stands there with a dumb look on her face.

There's blood.

The first thing that comes to Hager's hand is unwieldy, heavy, and very shiny.

Smack.

It comes down on Dorothea's head. There's no yes or no. Right or wrong or maybe.

She lands on the basement floor with a thud, dark stains blooming around her.

Hager guesses he won't have to worry about how many peanuts Dorothea eats anymore.

He wishes he'd borrowed a shovel from Albert as well.

Mother-Robber

"I don't know what to do about them, Albert."

Daphne is folding laundry in the front room. Through the net curtains, I see one shade of grey on another. A light drizzle has troubled us for days. My landlady picks petticoats and panties off a wooden clotheshorse, and forces the cardboard-stiff cotton into submission with a shake.

"Yes. I suppose they've been trouble from the start." I pull a pair of pale stockings from the frame and roll them into a ball, the way I have seen Daphne do so many times. I like to help. "What have they done now?" The doughnut-coloured hosiery in my hands has a snag in it. I hope it wasn't my doing. My nails are long, but I keep them filed, barbs smoothed away with an emery board, the way I've been taught.

"Not them. It's her. The girl, Pillar. Little vixen."

"Oh?" It's not like Daphne to be uncharitable. After all, she took *me* in didn't she? And I'm not the first one she rehabilitated from Armley High Security.

"She's been bringing roadkill into the house."

"Roadkill? Why?"

"I don't bloody know." Daphne folds a voluminous brassiere in half, one white cup in the other. "It was the smell that alerted me."

I must admit the house on Victoria Road has carried an odd odour in recent weeks, a hot cooked meat smell, but not in any way pleasant.

"Did you ask her about it? Or did you ask the mother? Surely Ines knows?"

"I went into their room when they were out."

My throat tightens. Though I come and go as I please, my bedsit is sacrosanct. There are things in there I'd prefer Daphne not to see. But if she's been snooping around in *their* room, the chances are —

"Can you go into tenants' rooms without permission?"

150

"You're a fine one to talk, Albert Timmins," she says. "You're always snooping around other people's rooms."

"Only if they leave them unlocked." That's a barefaced lie, so I don't respond further. Anyway, I want to know more about what Ines Watteau's brat has done that's bad enough to rattle Daphne. Daphne knows no fear. She's encountered everything in her long life. "What did you see?"

"The first thing I found looked like a weasel, though it might have been a stoat. I find it hard to tell them apart. It had dried out a bit."

"Children are curious." I say what I think I should, with little idea whether it's the right thing or not.

"Oh but there's more," Daphne continues. "The weasel was lying in a plant pot by the window. She'd wrapped its poor little body around the wax begonia Ines has."

"How do you know it was the girl who did it?"

"It has to be, because when I went into the alcove where Pillar's bed is, it stank like a pair of whore's drawers. I found more in a box by the bed."

"More what?"

"Animals. Dead ones. Oh Glory! The sight of them." Daphne raises her hand to her mouth. "Two fat maggots spilled over the edge when I lifted the lid."

"What sort of box? How big was it?"

"Wooden, a small trunk really. I don't know how she got it up there. And as for what was in it — there were some whole creatures, and some pieces of larger animals." Daphne shudders. I thought she was made of sterner stuff. I wonder if I should hold her hand, but Daphne warned me not to touch her after a recent episode in the toilet.

"What sort of animals?" I ask.

"I don't know. I didn't *touch* them. Though I thought I saw a deer antler poking through the mound of fur and rotting flesh." She makes a strange sound, as if she is swallowing backwards.

"Are you going to talk to Ines about it?"

"They're at church. I have to pick the right time. But there's more."

It gets worse. Daphne describes crackers arranged on a plate like sacramental bread, and an inverted crucifix.

What has Pillar been up to?

Ines Watteau and her child are a strange pair. No one in the house knows where the woman and her child came from, or how long they'll stay. There's a temporary air about them. The eight-year-old has wise-looking eyes, though I'm not sure she puts her wisdom to good use.

Ines supposedly sends the girl to the local school, but I often find her playing dominoes in the lounge mid-morning. I've heard the other tenants whisper the pair are versed in the dark arts. Ines will do you a Tarot reading for a small fee, and can read palms. Norman from the pub says he's seen her turning tricks by the railway station. She's on the benefit, what with no sign of a father for her child, or a steady job.

When Ines and the girl return, I'm waiting at the top of the stairs, peering through the bannisters, hoping to catch a glimpse of a confrontation with Daphne. But there is no sign of our landlady. Ines shakes her umbrella.

Quick as a flash, the girl's hand slips into the leather bag her mother has placed on the counter, while she pulls her raincoat off. The girl's hand is out in less than a second. She's tucked a paper note into her fist. It might be a fiver. It might be more.

"Come. Let's heat some soup on the stove," the mother says. "Warm your bones a little."

"Not now, Maman," the girl says. "I have to go out."

Before her mother can reply, the girl slips out of the door.

Daphne's right. It's not the mother we should be worrying about. Perhaps we should be worried *for* her.

Sorry

To patrons of the *Pig and Whistle* public house who were present on Sunday 25th November.

I, Patsy Weston, of 115 Victoria Road, apologise unreservedly for any offence I may have caused at the above-mentioned public house on Sunday night.

I apologise for attempting to strangle the gentleman in the white sports jacket with my underwear. You have the right to support whichever football team you wish.

To the lady from Llangollen, whom I assaulted with a plastic drinking straw and cocktail umbrella: You were right. A slippery nipple does contain Sambuca. I owe you one, and have left money behind the bar for said beverage when you're next in the area. And I'm sorry about the dress. I hadn't realised my chewing gum wasn't in my mouth anymore.

To my friend Michelle Timmins: you were right, your husband is rubbish in the sack.

To the man with the patched elbows, whom I assaulted just before closing time: sorry about the false teeth.

To Ronnie. Sorry, I didn't realise you were underage. I hope it will grow back eventually. You can't blame me entirely for this one, though. You did resemble the man on your fake I.D.

Furthermore, I apologise to all adherents of the Zoroastrian religion for insensitive comments I made regarding tower blocks and bad smells. Cremation is probably more suited to this part of the world, though. Don't get too many vultures in these parts.

Sincerely yours,
Patsy Weston (Mrs.)

P.S. If anyone finds a right fluoro-pink high-heeled shoe, size ten and a half, please be good enough to drop it off to Norman at the bar at the *Pig*.

The Covenant

Her mother folds a silk handkerchief into Mary's hand.

"Something old," she whispers, though not quietly enough.

After the ceremony, a flake of confetti slides from the ebony of my wife's hair. The flint-brightness of her eyes is celestial, her hands as small as a child's. I want to keep these memories forever. This is a love I cannot lose; yet inevitably I know I must, like the others. And somehow, I hope it will be different with Mary.

She wants a child, not just one.

"Strong strapping lads, like you, Albert," she tells me each month, when they fail to take, "and a girl, if we could have a girl, as precious as a pearl."

"In good time, my love," I say, though I know it will never happen.

Is it a lie, when you omit the truth? Is the promise of children obligatory in the covenant of marriage? Is it a betrayal, or just a misunderstanding on both our parts?

We spoke of children in abstract terms during our courtship, brief as it was, as so many are in these times of upheaval and recovery. And now, I hate myself when she takes the blame, sees herself as a barren woman.

They say only the good die young. That makes me far from good, yet I am not the devil. Others like me pass through to another realm, long before they have the chance of becoming fathers, but my covenant is different. It's one that sees me pass through the lives of others, to watch them grow old. I must leave them and move on, before they discover what I am.

Mary spends time with Desmond Waters, after he moves into the house opposite ours. There's a little silver in her hair now. I come home to find them sharing Rich Tea biscuits and a cup of tea.

"There's more in the pot if you want one, Albert," she says, but I want her to make me a fresh one. I've been at work all day. After all, what else has Mary got to do? The days when we needed all hands on deck to help with the war are over. She is a homemaker, feathering her empty nest. She squanders tears and compassion on this wastrel who has made himself comfortable in my armchair.

"It's just until he settles in," she says after Desmond leaves, washing the best china cups in suds. "He doesn't know anyone else in these parts."

I don't have to tell her I don't like it. She knows. There's more force in my lovemaking that night. I do it to show she is mine. She encourages me. Perhaps she thinks it will make my seed go further, penetrate the fortress at the entrance to her womb.

The situation doesn't improve over the months.

Desmond comes for dinner.

Desmond borrows a cup of sugar.

Desmond returns a cup of sugar.

Desmond asks Mary to show him around the market, so he can buy the best cuts of meat.

Desmond asks Mary to accompany him to the public library, so she can show him how to join.

She tells me she might find herself a little job. Something to keep her occupied while I'm at work, to earn a little money to put away for when we might need it.

I love her so much it makes my bones hurt.

I come home early one afternoon to find the house empty. The silence screams, mocking me. I was right. I need proof. Proof, then retribution. In the basement, my breath comes in harsh bursts as I select my tools. Following my instincts, I hold the axe low behind my back. Out of the house, across the road. I find the door open. Mary's coat hangs over a chair in the parlour, her shoes kicked off on the floor. Rock'n'roll music echoes from the gramophone. Mary is singing with the music, her voice sweet and lovely. The bedroom door is ajar. I step closer and hear her singing words of love. The rage grows inside me. I raise the axe, prepare to do what I must, my wife sings *I love you*. Before I can enter the room and surprise them, she steps out and I bring the axe down on her head. One. Two. Three.

She only screams once. Just once before the first blow.

Albert!

It's only when she is dead that I notice she is wearing her apron and house slippers. It's only when she is dead, that I see the cloth in her hand. And when I step into the room to finish her lover off, he enters the house through the front door.

"Yoo hoo! Hello Mrs. Timmins," he calls, climbing the stairs, and Desmond's mouth falls open when he sees me, axe by my hand, my wife at my feet.

The blood spreads to the top of the stairs.

A voice croons *I love you* on the gramophone.

Desmond screams in perfect harmony.

Hello

Dear Thakur Baba,

I came across your website whilst looking for something else. It was your picture that caught my eye. If I'm not mistaken, you also went by the name of Albert Timmins? Thought I'd say hello, in case it is you.

Now, let me see, it must be approaching forty years since we worked together, but you don't look a day older. You must let me know your secret. That is unless it is purely down to hot-hot yoga and the other principles you outline on your homepage, not some sort of pact with the devil, LOL.

I've attached a photo, but in case you are having trouble recognising me with all the greys, my name is Norman Wong. I used to work behind the bar of the *Pig and Whistle* when you were a glass collector there.

I always had a soft spot for you, Albert. You were a funny man, what with your singing and sage advice. I never believed all the stories I heard about you. I'll never forget the advice you gave me when I was having trouble in the bedroom department. Sprinkling nutmeg on my wife's pillow did nothing for my premature ejaculation, but it did make Lan Ying sneeze, which in turn had unexpected effects.

So, if it is you, I'm glad you seem to be doing well. Drop me a line, and perhaps we could meet for a beer, seeing as I am back in the district. We'll meet on the better side of the bar this time! I'd love to know how you are doing, and whether you ever got your memory back.

Oh, and I don't believe any of that stuff I read about your motivational posts on the *Snopes* page. Sour grapes, I'm sure.

Kind regards,
Your friend,
Norman Wong.

The Beginning and The End

"You were with me at the beginning." I push Ra's drink towards him and sip from my own. The whiskey tastes like kerosene. In truth, I've never drunk anything derived from petroleum products. I've drunk a lot worse though. "So what can I do for you?"

"I've come for the money."

"What money?"

"With compound interest, Albert." He pushes a sheet towards me. I scrutinise the tiny print, angry lines, black with red highlights. Itemised accounts for time stolen from the gods. "You can't run forever."

"I see." I pull my chair back, and step to the window. The sun is low in the sky. Fiery red wings tinged purple span the full width of my panoramic view. I can see everything from here, but I failed to see trouble coming.

Ra twists the amulet around his neck. There is an odour about him. It's not unpleasant, reminds me of better times. His musky sweetness, almost medicinal, takes me back to a time when we meant something altogether different to one another. Erasing the memory from my mind, I turn to face him.

"Did *he* send you?"

"Never mind who sent me, Albert. Your time is up."

"I thought I had eternity."

"Even eternity ends."

"I imagined it would happen differently." I open my drawer. My gun is still there. Surely Ra knows the danger he faces visiting me in my own territory. But could I kill him? He is like a brother to me. More, though stars have been born and more have died in the time since I held him — I dismiss the thought. And if I killed him, what then? My debt unpaid, it's only a matter of time until the others catch me. Time. I don't have time. The edges of the sky are tinged indigo. The light in my office no longer obeys the known laws of physics.

"You know you can't, Albert," he says, rising as I reach for the weapon. "Let's do this the easy way." The sound of planets moving in the distance distracts me, and Ra seizes the moment. He's upon me like a tidal wave, and the gun becomes flesh in my hand. I have become the weapon. It has become me.

"Did you think you could harm me?" he hisses.

I bare my teeth and growl at him. What does he think I am? A fucking mortal?

"Did you think you could harm me?" he asks again. Rhetorical. "I am Ra, who rose beneath the stars, son of Xavier. You owe a debt, Albert Timmins, and I mean to collect it."

That's when I jump to the ceiling, run across the tiles and smash through the plate glass window, fall faster, harder, and crash into Michelle's arms sweating, breathing hard.

"Fuckin' 'ell, Albert! Wot's up with ya?"

"Huh?"

"You nearly 'ad me eye out."

"He came. Came for the money."

"Who did?" She strokes my cheek. There are times my wife is almost tender.

"No one. Nothing." I squeeze her shoulder. "It was a dream."

But deep in my heart, I know it wasn't.

It's only a matter of time before everything falls apart, but I mean to have more. Oh yes, I mean to have more.

Fast and Slow

"So what brings you here?"

Petaluma sits in the concrete chair opposite me, and puffs on a biri. The pink-black smoke curls into the already ugly air.

"Thought I'd come see you before end-times, Bertie." They, and they always insisted I used the plural pronoun; they lift a booted foot onto my desk.

"Bull – " I grab their biri and suck myself a lungful, "– shit."

"What?" Their voice is as patronising as it always was.

"I ain't buying this end of the world bollocks. That's what ignorant people said at the start of the millennium." I extinguish Petaluma's biri, even though there's a good finger-length left. They give me a dark look. "And guess what? We're still here." I stand up and walk around them, take in the matted hair, down to their shoulders, the piteously sagging breasts, the short legs, chestnut smile. "And don't call me Bertie. No one calls me Bertie."

"Okay, *Albert*," they say. "You've been pedalling lies so long. Maybe you started to believe them yourself?" That self-satisfied smirk again. Were they always such a pain-in-the-arse? They take another smoke out of their jacket pocket and light up.

"What lies?" I ask, indignant.

"Tell me. What religion do you profess to be part of now? Brahmoism? Neo-Paganism? United Apostasy?"

Sonja comes in with a tray. I ask her to leave it on the table.

"What's it to you?" I take a cherry and spit the pip onto the floor.

"I've come to make you an offer." They lay a sheet of paper on the table beside the tray, pick up a grape, and toy with it, like they've never seen food before. I guess I owe it to them to listen. After all, we were once friends. More.

There aren't many like Petaluma and me. Guess that's a good thing. I suppose that's why we hung out together for so long. Being like we are doesn't mean you sit around and do nothing, waiting for nothing to happen. Sure, I wasn't always motivated the way I am now. Guess that's why Pet and I ended up living in the squat for so long.

But after a while, you want to do what other people do, even though you know you're not like them.

We had good times, Petaluma and I. They drove us from coast to coast, faster than the wind, so swift that I thought we'd split the atoms before us.

We'd go hunting for women together, though Pet wasn't as particular as me. *Anything goes when you're a hermaphrodite*, they'd say. Their words then as now, strangely twisted by the accent that came from the small Californian town they took their name from.

Why did things go sour between us?

Guess there was never a town big enough for two souls as complex as ours. Two souls trying to cream the locals for whatever we could get from them.

"Come back with me," Petaluma says. "Leave all this. The women, the guns, the cash. Come with me, and I'll guarantee you a good death."

"Death?" I push the paper towards them. I stand, though my fists are still on the table. "Who said anything about death?"

"Albert, we're all dying."

"No." But even as I say it, I know they are right. "No, my friend. I'm not ready to go."

"Did you think you'd go on for ever?" They unfold the document, and the room grows a shade darker.

I remember Mary, and the injustice I did my fifth wife. There is no afterlife. There is nothing after this. I think about Michelle, Minnie, a woman named February, and a musician called Jazzy who despised jazz. I remember all my wives and lovers. Half the room is black. It's slipping away.

"It's time, Albert." They take a fountain pen from their jacket and offer it to me.

"No," I tell them, but there is resignation in my words. The blackness fills the corners of my heart, forms curtains across my eyes.

"You must, Albert," Petaluma says. "Now, before it's too late."

The black extinguishes the final light and I am —

Psych Ward

"Who carked?" Thomas asks.
  "Albert Timmins."
  "How?"
  "Stroke."
  "Thought he was god, didn't he?"
  "Yeah. Immortal."
He steals a chip from my plate.
  "Got that wrong, didn't he?"

When Hope Has Died

I call out my father's name, but cannot give my words meaning. This is what happens at the end. This is the ultimate betrayal.

I contemplate how it has come to this.

Leaving on the longest day, a guest at my last summer.

I leave alone and friendless.

To be abandoned when hope has died.

All I feel now is all I will ever know: the chill of my feet, transubstantiation of the blood in my veins to water.

Acknowledgements

Eileen Merriman, critique partner extraordinaire, who breathes the fire of life into all the stories.

Nancy Stohlman, who created the prompts these stories came from, in the Flash Nano Facebook events 2016-8.

Matt Potter, for his encouragement and belief.

Heather Matthews, for offering a second pair of eyes, and for so much more.

Spelk Fiction, for publishing a version of *Misty* in June 2018.

About the Author

Nod Ghosh completed a creative writing course at the Hagley Writers' Institute in Christchurch, New Zealand in 2014. Her stories and poems have appeared in *Landfall*, *Takahē*, *JAAM*, and other New Zealand and overseas publications.

Anthologies featuring Nod's work include: *Love on the Road* and *Landmarks* (2015); *Leaving the Red Zone* (2016); *Sleep is A Beautiful Colour*, *True*, and *Wiser* (2017); *Happy²* (2018); and *Stories My Gay Uncle Told Me*, and *And We Pass Through* (2019).

The novella *The Crazed Wind* was published by Truth Serum Press, in 2018.

Nod's competition placements include:
• Runner up New Zealand National Flash Fiction Day, 2016.
• Runner up Bath Flash Fiction award, June 2017.
• Joint 1st place Wallace Foundation Creative Non Fiction Contest, 2018.
• Runner up North and South short short story competition, 2016 and 2018.

Nod was born in the U.K. and works as a medical laboratory scientist. The day job involves writing the truth, which is why it's such fun writing made up stuff at night.

Visit Nod's website at http://www.nodghosh.com/about/.

Also from TRUTH SERUM PRESS

https://truthserumpress.net/catalogue/

- *How to Catch Flathead* by Peter Michal
  978-1-925536-94-2 (paperback) 978-1-925536-95-9 (eBook)
- *The Last Free Man* by Lewis Woolston
  978-1-925536-88-1 (paperback) 978-1-925536-89-8 (eBook)
- *The Story of the Milkman* by Alan Walowitz
  978-1-925536-76-8 (paperback) 978-1-925536-77-5 (eBook)

- *Minotaur and Other Stories* by Salvatore Difalco
  978-1-925536-79-9 (paperback) 978-1-925536-80-5 (eBook)
- *Easy Money* by Steve Evans
  978-1-925536-81-2 (paperback) 978-1-925536-82-9 (eBook)
- *The Book of Acrostics* by John Lambremont, Sr.
  978-1-925536-52-2 (paperback) 978-1-925536-53-9 (eBook)

Also from TRUTH SERUM PRESS

https://truthserumpress.net/catalogue/

- *Square Pegs* by Rob Walker
  978-1-925536-62-1 (paperback) 978-1-925536-63-8 (eBook)
- *Cheat Sheets* by Edward O'Dwyer
  978-1-925536-60-7 (paperback) 978-1-925536-61-4 (eBook)
- *The Crazed Wind* by Nod Ghosh
  978-1-925536-58-4 (paperback) 978-1-925536-59-1 (eBook)

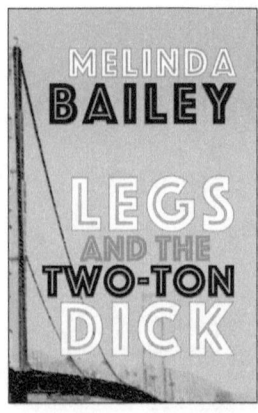  

- *Legs and the Two-Ton Dick* by Melinda Bailey
  978-1-925536-37-9 (paperback) 978-1-925536-38-6 (eBook)
- *Dollhouse Masquerade* by Samuel E. Cole
  978-1-925536-43-0 (paperback) 978-1-925536-44-7 (eBook)
- *Kiss Kiss* by Paul Beckman
  978-1-925536-21-8 (paperback) 978-1-925536-22-5 (eBook)

Also from TRUTH SERUM PRESS

https://truthserumpress.net/catalogue/

- *Inklings* by Irene Buckler
  978-1-925536-41-6 (paperback) 978-1-925536-42-3 (eBook)
- *On the Bitch* by Matt Potter
  978-1-925536-45-4 (paperback) 978-1-925536-46-1 (eBook)
- *Too Much of the Wrong Thing* by Claire Hopple
  978-1-925536-33-1 (paperback) 978-1-925536-34-8 (eBook)

- *Track Tales* by Mercedes Webb-Pullman
  978-1-925536-35-5 (paperback) 978-1-925536-36-2 (eBook)
- *Luck and Other Truths* by Richard Mark Glover
  978-1-925101-77-5 (paperback) 978-1-925536-04-1 (eBook)
- *Hello Berlin!* by Jason S. Andrews
  978-1-925536-11-9 (paperback) 978-1-925536-12-6 (eBook)

Also from TRUTH SERUM PRESS

https://truthserumpress.net/catalogue/

 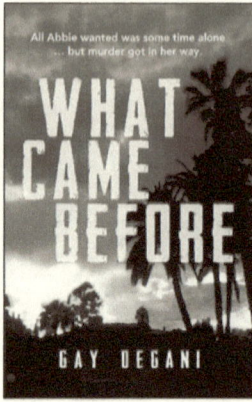 

- *Deer Michigan* by Jack C. Buck
  978-1-925536-25-6 (paperback) 978-1-925536-26-3 (eBook)
- *What Came Before* by Gay Degani
  978-1-925536-05-8 (paperback) 978-1-925536-06-5 (eBook)
- *Rain Check* by Levi Andrew Noe
  978-1-925536-09-6 (paperback) 978-1-925536-10-2 (eBook)

 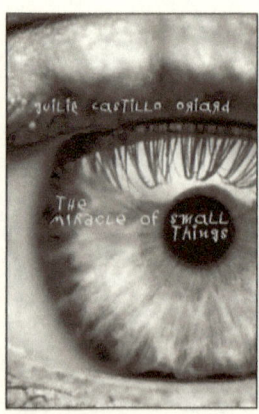 

- *Based on True Stories* by Matt Potter
  978-1-925101-75-1 (paperback) 978-1-925101-76-8 (eBook)
- *The Miracle of Small Things* by Guilie Castillo Oriard
  978-1-925101-73-7 (paperback) 978-1-925101-74-4 (eBook)
- *La Ronde* by Townsend Walker
  978-1-925101-64-5 (paperback) 978-1-925101-65-2 (eBook)

www.ingramcontent.com/pod-product-compliance
Lightning Source LLC
Chambersburg PA
CBHW020615250626
47154CB00004B/1517